Ranger's revenge
LP-WF Gri   T47399

Mediapolis Public Library

elp us Rate this book...
ut your initials on the
ft side and your rating
on the right side.
1 = Didn't care for
2 = It was O.K.
3 = It was <u>great</u>

DATE DUE

MAR 2 4 2013			
APR - 9 2013			
MAY - 2 2013			
AUG 2 1 2018			
JAN 1 4 2020 LH			

eM   1 2 3
dru   1 2 3
mc.   1 2 3
_____   1 2 3
_____   1 2 3
_____   1 2 3
_____   1 2 3
_____   1 2 3
_____   1 2 3
_____   1 2 3
_____   1 2 3
_____   1 2 3
_____   1 2 3
_____   1 2 3
_____   1 2 3

PRINTED IN U.S.A.

D1444634

Ranger's Revenge

Center Point
Large Print

Also by James J. Griffin and available from
Center Point Large Print:

Death Stalks the Rangers
Death Rides the Rails

RANGER'S REVENGE

A Texas Ranger Jim Blawcyzk Story

James J. Griffin

CENTER POINT LARGE PRINT
THORNDIKE, MAINE

This Center Point Large Print edition is published in the year 2018 by arrangement with the author.

The text of this Large Print edition is unabridged. In other aspects, this book may vary from the original edition. Printed in the United States of America on permanent paper. Set in 16-point Times New Roman type.

ISBN: 978-1-68324-690-9

Library of Congress Cataloging-in-Publication Data

Names: Griffin, James J., 1949- author.
Title: Ranger's revenge : a Texas Ranger Jim Blawcyzk story / James J. Griffin.
Description: Center Point large print edition. | Thorndike, Maine : Center Point Large Print, 2018.
Identifiers: LCCN 2017050650 | ISBN 9781683246909 (hardcover : alk. paper)
Subjects: LCSH: Texas Rangers—Fiction. | Large type books.
Classification: LCC PS3607.R5477 R36 2018 | DDC 813/.6—dc23
LC record available at https://lccn.loc.gov/2017050650

For Debbie McConnell and her mustang, Joya, my Horse Patrol and trail riding pards.

As always, I express my gratitude to Paul Dellinger for his invaluable suggestions.

Prologue

"Jim, where are you going? It must be two in the morning."

Julia Blawcyzk looked at her husband Jim, a lieutenant in the Texas Rangers, as he sat up and swung his legs over the edge of their bed.

"I think Candy's about to have her foal," Jim answered. He fumbled for a lucifer, struck it, and lit the lamp on the bedside table.

"What makes you think that?" Julia asked.

"You said this evening she probably wouldn't have it for another day or two."

"Listen."

"I don't hear anything."

"The horses are restless out there, and I heard Sonny whinnyin' a couple of minutes ago." Jim tugged on his jeans and socks, pulled on his boots, and shrugged into his shirt. "Why do they always have their babies in the middle of the night?"

"Women have been asking that same question for years," Julia said laughing. "You'll recall Charlie arrived at four in the morning. It was a warm night when he decided to enter the world too, just like tonight."

"And Charlie kept waking us up at four in

the morning for weeks afterwards," Jim said grinning.

"He surely did. I'll make some coffee and bring it out to you."

"You don't need to go to that trouble," Jim answered. He jammed his Stetson over his unruly shock of thick blond hair. "This might just be a false alarm. I'll come back and let you know once I'm certain. There's no point in both of us losing sleep."

Tiptoeing to avoid waking their nine year old son, Charlie, Jim crossed the kitchen and stepped onto the porch. Outside, he increased his pace. When he neared the stable, two handsome paint horses in separate corrals lifted their heads and neighed to him.

"Looks like you're gonna be a dad soon, Sonny?" Jim said to the sorrel overo stallion pacing back and forth. Jim patted the horse's nose when the big stud came up to the fence and nickered to him. He paused at the next corral to stroke the neck of the palomino splotched tobiano gelding hanging his head over the fence and whickering to him. Sam, his Ranger mount and equine partner of many trails, was a one-man animal whose sharp teeth and hooves had saved his rider's life on more than one occasion.

"You just take it easy, pard," he told Sam while the horse nuzzled his shoulder. "We'll be back on the trail soon enough."

Jim headed into the barn, took a lucifer from his shirt pocket and struck it. He removed a lantern from its wall bracket, lifted the chimney, and touched the match to the wick. Once the light took hold, Jim held the lantern toward a roomy stall which held a sorrel mare. The horse was stretched out on her side in the final throes of labor. She groaned with her efforts.

Jim knelt alongside the mare, stroked her neck and whispered to her. "Easy, Candy. It won't be long now."

Jim remained with the mare, continuing to stroke her neck while the contractions intensified and became more frequent. He turned at a slight sound behind him to find his wife and son standing there.

"How close is she?" asked Julia balancing two mugs of steaming coffee in her hands. Beside her, Charlie stood wide-eyed.

"Any minute now," Jim answered.

Candy nickered with pain, and then her body shuddered as it was wracked by the strongest contraction yet.

"Here it comes," Jim said when the foal's head appeared. A few moments later a sorrel colt with overo markings made his entry into the world.

"It's a stud colt," he said.

"And he's a real beauty," Julia added.

"Wow!" was all Charlie could manage.

Candy went to work licking and nuzzling her newborn son, urging him to his feet.

Once the newborn stood on wobbly legs and began nursing, Jim said, "Let's leave them alone for a while. We'll turn them out in the corral for a bit come morning."

"Which it already is," Julia said.

"I reckon it is." Jim smiled. "Well, later this morning."

After a couple more hours of sleep, Jim rolled out of bed and trudged back to the barn where he fed the horses and checked on Candy and her new son. Satisfied all was well he returned to the house for breakfast. Once he and his family had eaten they headed for the barn.

Jim haltered the mare and led her, with her colt following along, to the corral behind Sonny's, where he turned her loose. Sonny whinnied proudly as he watched his new son take a few tentative steps around the corral. The long-legged foal was a handsome sorrel color which glistened in the bright Texas sun like a newly minted copper penny. He had a bald face, white stockings to his knees on his forelegs and a white marking on the inside of the left foreleg between knee and shoulder. His hind legs were white to the hocks, with the white continuing up the front of the legs to his flanks. Large white patches extending from his belly up his ribs, midway on his right side and just behind his left shoulder, contrasted with the bold sorrel coloring. A white spot resembling a downward pointing arrowhead on the left side of his neck, in front of the shoulder, completed his unique markings.

Already feeling bold the colt scampered away from his mother and headed straight for Jim to tug on the Ranger's shirtsleeve with his gums. When Jim broke out laughing, the colt raced away. He ran along the fence before heading back to his mother to do some serious nursing.

"That's going to be your horse, Jim," Julia observed.

"Better not let Sam know," Jim answered. His long-time trail partner was pacing in his own corral and whickering to his rider.

"He needs a name," said Charlie.

"How about you giving him one?" Jim replied. "Do you have anything in mind?"

The colt backed away from his mother, kicking up his heels and dashing around the corral.

"He runs so fast he sizzles," Charlie said, "And it's a sizzling hot day already. His name's gonna be Sizzle."

"Then Sizzle it is," Jim agreed.

Chapter 1

Four Years Later

"Just about time to quit for the night. Your mom should have supper almost ready," Jim told Charlie. He and his son had been working all day at getting a wagonload of hay into the barn's loft before an approaching storm hit.

Jim jumped from the now-empty buckboard. He untied the bandanna from his neck to wipe sweat from his face and chest. Charlie did the same. He worshipped his lawman father, and often imitated Jim's every move. In the blistering late July heat, father and son had removed their drenched shirts and hung them from the buckboard's tailgate. It was far more comfortable to work stripped to their waists than with the heavy, sweat-soaked garments clinging to their backs. And out here on the JB Bar, their small horse ranch, it was highly unlikely any "proper" society woman would happen by to be shocked at seeing the bare-chested pair. In fact, Julia had noted that very fact when she brought out their noontime dinner.

"Jim, do you realize you and Charlie would horrify most of the town women if they saw you two parading around half-naked like that?" she had teased.

"Do you have any objections to us bein' shirtless?" Jim had answered.

"Why, none at all." Julia had touched a finger to the tip of Jim's nose, letting it trail down through the thick blonde hair covering his chest. "In fact, I'm enjoying the view. I suspect most of those so-called proper women secretly would too. Now you enjoy your dinner. I've got some mending to do."

With the day's work now over, Jim smiled at the promise he'd seen in his wife's eyes and felt in her gentle touch.

"What're you grinnin' about, Dad?" Charlie asked.

"Nothin' in particular. Let's get to supper," Jim answered.

"It's about time, Dad. I'm starved." Charlie grinned.

At the age of thirteen, the boy had shot up over the past few months. He now stood nearly as tall as his six-foot plus father. Though his muscles still had the stringiness of early adolescence, Charlie's approaching manhood had begun to thicken his lanky frame. With blonde hair and clear blue eyes that were exact matches for his father's he could almost be taken for Jim's kid brother.

"Let's wash up," Jim said.

He and Charlie hurried to the pump and wash bench between the house and barn. They began cleaning up, ducking their heads in the cool water of the trough. Without warning, Charlie punched Jim playfully in his belly.

"C'mon, Dad. Let's wrestle. Bet I can take you this time," he challenged.

"Maybe later," Jim answered. "Right now I'm ready to eat."

Charlie punched his dad in the belly again, a bit harder. "What's the matter, Dad? You gettin' old? Turnin' yella? Afraid you'll lose?"

"Not a chance of that," Jim replied. He returned his son's favor, sinking his fist into Charlie's gut just hard enough so that the boy doubled over a little bit. Charlie's knees buckled, and Jim wrapped an arm around his neck.

"Now we'll see who's yellow," Jim growled in feigned anger. "Get ready to be pounded into the dirt, kid."

Charlie shot a backhanded slap to his father's stomach and twisted out of Jim's grasp.

"You'll have to catch me first, Dad," he taunted. Charlie raced across the dusty yard with Jim in hot pursuit.

Charlie made it almost to the fence before Jim caught up with him. The big Ranger's diving tackle sent both of them plunging to the dirt, rolling over and over. They came to a stop with Jim on his back, his son sprawled across his stomach.

"I've got'cha, Dad," Charlie yelled, twisting around to pin Jim's shoulders.

"Not so fast, young 'un." Jim pushed hard against Charlie's stomach, flipping the boy over. Jim scrambled to drop across his son's chest. "Now who's got who?" he rumbled. "Give up?"

"Not yet." Charlie wrapped his arms around Jim's back and rolled.

For several minutes they battled, neither father nor son able to gain an advantage or willing to give an inch. They were so engrossed in their battle that they failed to hear Julia approaching until she dumped a bucket of cold water over them.

Jim and Charlie yelped with shock when the icy water hit their overheated flesh.

"Mom! What'd you do that for?" Charlie remained flopped on his back.

"I've been calling the both of you to supper for the last fifteen minutes, but you were so engrossed in your horseplay you never heard me. That was the only way I could get your attention. Y'all are impossible. One of you could get hurt."

His chest heaving as he gasped for breath, Jim pushed himself to his feet. Trying to look sheepish, he tried one of his crooked smiles on her. "We were just havin' some fun, darlin'. There's no harm done."

"There's no harm done as long as you don't mind eating a burnt roast and dried out potatoes. Supper's ruined."

"Aw honey, you know I like things cooked until they're almost burnt anyway. I'm sure the roast will be just fine."

Jim tried to wrap his arms around his wife's waist.

"Don't even think of that," Julia said, glaring at him. "The two of you are filthy from rolling around in the dirt while you're all sweaty. You must be covered with an inch of mud. You'll both take a bath before either of you come into my clean kitchen."

"But the tub's in the house, Mom!" Charlie protested. "And by the time we drag it out and fill it supper will really be cold."

"Who said anything about using the tub?" Julia answered. "You two can just scrub in the stock tank by the windmill. I'll bring soap and towels out to you."

"But Mom, the horses drink from that tank. We can't get soap in their water."

"That tank's full, and it's going to rain tonight, so the water will be fresh by morning," Julia pointed out. "And you've bathed in that tank before, Charles William Blawcyzk. Of course there's always the stream. It's up to you, and your incorrigible father. But you're both taking that bath."

16

"We can't win, Charlie," Jim said with a sigh. "All right, Julia, it's the tank for us."

Later that evening, Julia and Jim were sitting in the porch swing, listening to the rain spattering on the roof. As Julia rested her head on Jim's shoulder, she idly ran a hand through his thick blonde hair.

"You seem awfully quiet tonight, Jim," she said. "Is something bothering you?"

"Not a thing," Jim answered, "I'm just listening to the rain. After the dry spell we've had it's a wonderful sound."

"Jim, we've been together too long for you to try and fool me. There's something on your mind."

"It's just that with Charlie's collie dying last month and us going to get him a new puppy tomorrow, well, that's got me to thinking."

"Thinking about what, dear?"

"About Sam. He's getting on in years, and I'm going to have to retire him soon. I still haven't found the right horse to take his place. And Sam's sure not going to be happy the first time I ride out and leave him behind."

"What about Sizzle? That horse adores you, and you said yourself he's got the makings of a good Ranger's horse."

Over the last four years, Sizzle had grown into an exceptional animal. At sixteen hands high and

17

powerfully built with long legs, the horse showed speed, staying power and high intelligence.

"I know," Jim agreed. "But he's too mellow. Nothing seems to bother him. With Sam I always knew if anybody was around, like maybe a bushwhacker waitin' to put a bullet in my back. Sizzle doesn't look for anything like that. He's so easygoin' nothing fazes him. And he's just too doggone friendly. He wants to visit with everybody he sees. Plus he's such a handsome fella he catches everyone's eye. Add to that his speed and strength and he's horse thief bait. He'll get himself stolen before we're on the trail a month."

"Jim, I would think after all those years of riding that ornery Sam it would be a pleasant change having a mount you didn't have to warn everyone away from." Julia snuggled up closer to her husband. "I know you and he have been together a long time, but Sam's temper must make things difficult."

"It does, but Sam and I have been trail pards for so long I just can't face the thought of being out there without him." Jim closed his eyes and sighed. "Of course, the livery stable owners would be relieved. So would most of the other Rangers."

"I wouldn't worry too much for now," Julia said. "You'll know the right horse when it comes along. And it will be some time yet before you have to leave Sam behind."

"Yeah, I reckon so."

"I'll take your mind off that problem for now." Julia pressed her lips to his but received no kiss in return.

A lightning flash illuminated the porch for a split second, followed by a huge clap of thunder. "The wind's gettin' stronger. Rain's pickin' up too," Jim said.

"Thunderstorms always are exciting," Julia answered. "And you can't do anything about a horse tonight anyway. Let's just sit out here and watch the storm."

Jim fretted as a heavy gust rattled the windows. "I just hope the windmill doesn't tear itself apart in this wind. I didn't realize it was going to be this hard of a blow. I should have disconnected the mechanism."

"You can't do anything about that either," Julia pointed out.

"I guess you're right."

"You know I am," Julia whispered. She snuggled closer.

Chapter 2

The previous night's storm had settled the dust, giving the land a just-washed appearance. A light north wind gave the air an earthy tang. Jim noticed something amiss as soon as he went to feed the horses. Despite the breeze, the windmill was not turning. Jim crossed the pasture to examine it.

"Doggone it," he muttered when he looked up at the mechanism, "Storm must've loosened one of the gears, maybe the pinion. Looks like it bent a couple of the blades too. I'll have to get right on this."

Julia was standing on the porch as Jim hurried back for some tools. "Jim, breakfast is just about ready," she called.

"It's gotta wait a while. The windmill's busted. I've got to fix it."

"A half hour while you eat won't make any difference. Or would you rather have cold hotcakes?"

"I reckon you're right."

Jim washed up and headed inside to join his wife and son for the morning meal.

Once breakfast was finished, Jim and Charlie got the needed tools from the barn and headed to the windmill.

"We're goin' for my new pup today, aren't we Dad?" Charlie asked on the way. "You promised."

"We sure are, Charlie." Jim grinned and tousled his son's blonde hair. "Soon as we get this contraption workin' again, we'll saddle the horses and head over to Mr. Hines' place."

Jim peeled off his shirt and hung it from one of the windmill's cross braces. Unbuckling his gunbelt, he hung it alongside the shirt. He shoved hammer, wrench, and screwdrivers behind his belt and began his climb.

"Found the problem," Jim shouted down to Charlie as soon as he reached the top of the mill's tower. "Wind bent a couple of the blades, and they jammed the gears. I'll have it fixed right quick. Why don't you start gettin' the horses ready?"

"Sure thing, dad."

Charlie headed for the corrals to fetch Sam and his own gelding, Ted.

Jim hooked a knee over one of the timbers to brace himself and pulled the hammer from behind his belt. He was about to swing at one of the bent blades when a rifle slug smashed into his back, knocking him off the windmill's tower. His boot caught in a cross brace for a few seconds, holding him suspended in mid-air. Another bullet ricocheted across the top of his skull, sending a wave of blinding pain through his head. His body pulled loose and plummeted, landing stomach first on the edge of the wooden stock tank. The tank's wall collapsed under the impact. Jim's body hurtled across the yard propelled by the water rushing from the tank. The flow subsided quickly, leaving him sprawled in the mud.

Charlie raced from behind the barn at the sound of the shots. He saw his father lying face-down and unmoving.

"Dad!" he screamed.

The sound of approaching hoof beats caught his attention. He looked up to see a group of riders, guns at the ready, topping the rise overlooking the Blawcyzk ranch. Running to the windmill Charlie pulled his father's Colt Peacemaker from its holster. He snapped off one shot. His bullet took an oncoming raider in the stomach. The rider sagged over his horse's neck, clinging to its mane until the hard-running roan's motion spilled him from the saddle.

Another of the riders leveled his rifle and fired. A slug tore into Charlie's chest. He spun, staggered for a few feet, and fell face-down alongside his father.

The riders galloped into the ranch yard.

"Sure made our job easier with that Ranger bein' such a nice plain target up on that windmill," one of them said. He spat into the dirt alongside Blawcyzk's body.

"Never mind that. Let's just get the stock and get outta here," the leader of the renegades ordered. "A couple of you pick up Smitty and get him on his horse."

The outlaw Charlie had gut-shot was writhing in anguish where he'd fallen.

"What about the woman?" another asked. "Blawcyzk's got a real good-lookin' wife."

The leader grinned in anticipation. "Yeah, I reckon we'd better take care of her too. She's gotta be around here somewhere."

As if in answer, Julia appeared in the doorway, holding Jim's Winchester. Instantly one of the outlaws leveled his revolver and fired, his bullet striking the rifle. Julia lost her grasp on the gun as the bullet's impact slammed her back into the door frame. Her head struck the corner of the frame, stunning her. She slumped to the porch floor.

The leader dropped from his horse and headed for the house. "You boys round up the stock," he said. "Once I'm done with the woman you can have what's left of her."

"You want to burn the buildings, boss?"

"No! The smoke would attract someone's attention. That'd bring 'em down on us too fast. We've done what we set out to do, kill Jim Blawcyzk. Now round up those horses. We need to be ridin' in half an hour."

Chapter 3

Jim awakened to a severe pounding in his head and excruciating pain in his back. Fighting the nausea which threatened to overwhelm him, he pushed himself to his hands and knees.

"Charlie!" Jim called when he saw his son lying in the dirt. Jim's pistol was still clutched in Charlie's right hand. He rolled the boy onto his back. Bile rose in his throat when he saw the blood spreading over Charlie's shirt. He ripped opened the garment to reveal the bullet hole in his son's right breast. Jim studied the boy for a moment, relieved to see the shallow rising and falling of Charlie's chest. He pulled the bandanna from his neck, folded it, and placed it over the oozing wound. Prying Charlie's fingers from around the handle of his pistol Jim shoved it into the waistband of his own jeans.

"I need help. Gotta find Julia," Jim muttered.

Hoping Julia was somehow still safe, Jim staggered to his feet and lurched toward the house. "Julia! Where are you?" He called.

He struggled up the steps, nearly tripping over the ruined Winchester lying where Julia had dropped it, and into the house. He stopped short, struck speechless. Julia was lying unconscious in the middle of the kitchen floor. Her face was battered almost beyond recognition. Her clothes were torn and disheveled, revealing deep bruises over her body. Blood was splattered over the floor and walls, chairs were overturned and dishes broken. A piece of cloth ripped from one of her assailant's shirts was clutched in her hand, along with some strands of sandy-colored hair. Julia had apparently put up a ferocious fight against her attackers.

Despite his wounds, Jim managed to lift Julia from the floor and carry her to the living room. He placed her gently on the sofa, then pulled the cloth remnant and hair from her hand and slipped them into his pocket. He covered her with a quilt.

"I've got to ride for help, Julia," Jim hoarsely whispered. "I'll be back as quick as I can."

Burning with the desire for revenge, Jim stumbled down the steps and across the yard. Instinctively he knew this attack was the work of more than one man.

When Jim reached the barn he discovered the horses gone. Even Ben and Jerry, the draft horses, were missing. "Those sidewinders must've rustled 'em," he said. "They might've run off all the rest, but they'd never be able to run Sam off."

He whistled, and was answered by a weak whinny from the back corral. Jim hurried as best he could around the barn, every step sending pain ripping through him. The corral gate stood open. Sam was lying on his side, covered with blood. His left foreleg was bent at an odd angle. He whickered to Jim when the Ranger came into view. The big paint struggled to rise but fell back with a loud sigh. "Sam," Jim said kneeling beside the stricken animal. "You didn't let them take you, old feller! I knew you'd never let that happen."

Dangling from a splintered rail of Sam's corral were the bloody, shredded remains of a man's shirt. A ruined Stetson lay crushed in the dirt. Evidently one of the raiders had tried to take the big gelding, and had paid dearly for his attempt.

Jim pulled the Peacemaker from his belt.

"We've been down a lot of trails together, old pard, but I guess we've taken our last ride. I sure owe you a lot. And if the Lord's willing, I'll be ridin' you again someday across His green pastures."

Jim pointed the heavy pistol at Sam's head, then lowered it, unwilling to do what he knew had to be done. Sam had been Jim's trail partner for his entire Ranger career. They had traveled thousands of miles over the length and breadth of the Lone Star State. Saved from his abusive previous owner by Jim, Sam was a one-man animal, loyal only to the Ranger. Anyone else, except for Jim's wife and son, who attempted to even touch the palomino and white splotched gelding would be sure to feel the wrath of Sam's teeth and hooves. Those same teeth and hooves had saved Jim's life on more than one occasion. And even after all these years Sam's stamina and speed were hardly diminished.

Yet despite his vicious temper, Sam was gentle as a kitten with Jim. And everyone who met the pair quickly learned about Sam's insatiable sweet tooth. Jim always kept a supply of peppermints in his saddlebags and several in his hip pocket for his equine friend.

Tears streaming down his cheeks, Jim raised his pistol again, thumbed back the hammer of the Colt, and aimed it just behind Sam's ear. He pulled the trigger, and as the gun exploded he crumpled alongside his horse.

Chapter 4

Dully, Jim became aware of a horse's soft nose rubbing at his face, while some hard object kept striking his side, sending sharp pain stabbing through his injured ribs. His eyes flickered open. He found himself gazing up at Sam's muzzle.

"Sam!" Jim exclaimed in shock. Somehow the severely wounded gelding had managed to regain his feet. Hearing Jim's voice, Sam nuzzled more insistently at him. Several drops of blood ran off Sam's nose to splatter on Jim's face.

The Ranger was struck hard in his side yet again.

"Sizzle!" The young gelding was alongside Sam. He pawed once more at Jim's side. Jim grunted when the horse's hoof hit those sore ribs.

Despite his injuries, the Ranger managed a rueful chuckle. "I guess I'd better get off the ground before you two do what those *hombres* couldn't, and finish me off for good."

Jim picked up his gun and shoved it in the waistband of his jeans, then pulled himself to his feet. He gave the two horses a quick look. Sizzle had a length of lariat wrapped around his neck, which was scraped raw from the rope's rubbing against his hide. Evidently he had fought his captors until he managed to escape and head home.

Sam's injuries were far more serious. He still held his left foreleg at an unnatural angle and refused to put any weight on it. If the leg didn't have a broken bone, as it appeared, it certainly had a severely bowed tendon or torn ligaments. The big paint had a bullet wound in his right shoulder and another in his left hip. In addition, he had a crease where Jim's bullet had torn across the top of his head. Mercifully, when Jim collapsed his shot had missed its target.

Jim scratched both horses' ears. "Lord, I guess maybe it's not time for You to take Sam after all," he said. "Thanks for leavin' him here with me, and especially for causin' my bullet to miss. I'm more grateful than I can ever tell You. St. Francis, I'd sure appreciate it if you'd watch after Sam for me until I get back." Jim hesitated before adding with a soft laugh, "Of course, Sam, maybe you're just too doggone ornery for the Lord to want you quite yet."

Sam snorted.

"I can't take the time to care for you fellers," Jim said. "I've got to get the doc for Julia and Charlie. Sizzle, you're gonna have to get me there."

Realizing in his condition there was no way he could pull himself onto the tall gelding's back from the ground, Jim picked up the trailing length of rope around Sizzle's neck and led him to the fence. Sam limped after them.

The lawman's instinct took hold when Jim reached the fence. He pulled the torn, bloody shirt from the post and picked up the crushed Stetson.

"I'd better put these where they'll be safe. Might be the clue I need to track down these *hombres*," he muttered. He carried the shirt and hat into the barn and tucked them behind the grain bin.

Sizzle was still waiting patiently alongside the fence for the Ranger when Jim returned to the corral.

"Sam, I'll be back quick as I can, then I'll take care of you, old pardner," Jim told the paint, with a pat to his nose.

Jim pushed the thought that he would most likely still have to put Sam down to the back of his mind. He climbed the first two rails of the fence and swung onto Sizzle's bare back, wincing with the effort. He wrapped his hands in the horse's mane and heeled him into motion.

Sam nickered when Jim walked Sizzle slowly out of the corral. He hobbled over to Charlie and nuzzled the fallen youngster. The big paint nickered again, and then stood motionless alongside Charlie.

"Thanks, Sam," Jim called. "I don't have the strength to carry Charlie to the house. I know you'll watch over him while I'm gone, 'ol pard." He pushed Sizzle into a trot, then a smooth lope.

Jim headed for the nearest place he knew help would be available, the small ranch of his Texas Ranger partner, Smoky McCue. By the time he reached the McCue place Jim was slumped over Sizzle's neck, barely conscious and struggling to hang on. He had been forced to slow the paint's pace to a shuffling walk to avoid sliding off Sizzle's bare back. Jim called out weakly when his horse halted at the porch rail.

"Smoky!"

A moment later Smoky's wife, Cindy Lou, opened the front door.

"Jim? Is that you? What brings you by? Smoky's not home. He's . . ."

She stopped short when she spotted the half-naked Ranger sagging over his horse's neck. Blood caked Jim's scalp and was oozing down his back.

Cindy Lou hurried off the porch. "Jim! You're hurt! What happened to you?"

"I've been shot," Jim answered. He slid from Sizzle's back. "Charlie was shot too, and Julia . . . well, Julia's hurt real bad. I need the doc at my place fast."

"You need the doctor right here!" Cindy Lou said. "Let me help you into the house and I'll go fetch him from town. Sheriff Justus too."

She grabbed Jim's arm and draped it over her shoulders just before he collapsed.

"Gotta send him to help Julia and Charlie first," Jim whispered. "I'll be okay. Just get Doc Vender to them."

"Let me settle you and I'll do just that, I promise."

Cindy Lou helped Jim up the stairs and into the house.

"Just lie here on the sofa," she said.

"I'll get blood on it," Jim protested.

"Do you really think I'm worried, Jim Blawcyzk? You just lie down. I'll be right back."

Before Jim could object, she turned and hurried into the kitchen.

He dropped face-down on the sofa.

Cindy Lou returned with a folded towel and blanket in her arms. "I'm going to try and slow that bleeding." She placed the towel over the bullet hole in Jim's back, then spread the blanket over him.

"Where's Smoke?" Jim asked.

"Still up at Denton. Mack Mason's trial's taking longer than expected, so he didn't get home yesterday like he'd planned. He's still waiting to testify."

Cindy Lou tucked the blanket tightly around the wounded Ranger.

"I'm going for the doctor now. Don't you pull

anything stupid like getting off that sofa and trying to go after whoever did this," she ordered.

"That . . . thought never crossed . . . my mind," Jim murmured.

"Don't try and tell me that. I know you only too well, Jim Blawcyzk."

She hesitated, expecting a further objection, but none came. Jim had again passed out.

Cindy Lou ran to the barn and threw a saddle and bridle on her bay mare. She led the horse out of the stable and mounted. "Quickly, Dolly. You've got to run like you've never run before." She jabbed her heels into the mare's ribs, and the startled horse leapt forward at a dead run.

Chapter 5

When Jim awakened, he was lying on his stomach on a bed in a dimly lit room. Clean sheets covered his body. Half of the hair had been shaved from his scalp. He could feel the pressure of the bandages taped across his head and to his back. The mingled scents of soap, disinfectant, and medicines permeated the air. Jim recognized his surroundings. He had been in this room at Doctor Ronald Vender's small clinic many times. Vender was the sole physician in the area of San Leanna.

Jim lifted his head and glanced around the tidy room. Lying in the bed next to his was Charlie covered with blankets to his chin. Jim tried to push himself up, but dropped back to the mattress as a wave of nausea and vertigo overcame him. The room spun and he slipped back into unconsciousness.

The sound of the door being opened woke Jim up. He rolled onto his side and opened his eyes.

"Jim. I didn't expect to see you awake yet," said Dr. Vender as he walked over to the Ranger's bedside. "It's a good sign." He began to pull back Jim's covers.

"Never mind about me, Doc," Jim said.

"Where's my wife? And how's Charlie doing?"

Dr. Vender ran a hand through his wavy, steel-gray hair. "Julia's in the next room, doing as well as can be expected," he said. "I can say the same for Charlie."

"What's that mean?"

"Just what I said," Dr. Vender replied. "Julia was very badly beaten and she was raped. There's no polite way to say that. Besides her obvious injuries, she suffered a serious concussion. She's still unconscious. I expect her to eventually recover physically from the assault. But until she regains consciousness, there is no way of knowing whether she will have any permanent brain damage. And there is also no way to tell how the attack might affect her mental well-being."

"That's all you can tell me?"

"I'm sorry, Jim. I wish I could say Julia will be fine. But it's just too soon to know."

"What about Charlie?"

"Again, it's too soon to tell," Dr. Vender sat down beside Jim.

"Did you at least get the bullet out of his chest?"

"I did. The bullet went nearly right through him. I removed it through his back," Vender explained. "And luckily it struck high enough that it missed his lung. But your boy's wound is still extremely serious. The main worry right now is infection or blood poisoning. If either sets in then Charlie's chance of survival is poor. I don't have to tell you that."

"Any idea how soon you'll know?"

"Not really. It could be several days or several weeks. A pocket of infection could develop that wouldn't show for quite some time."

"All right, Doc. All we can do is wait," Jim said. "But I want to see Julia."

"In a day or two, perhaps. Right now you are far too weak to get out of that bed," Vender answered.

"Doc, I want to see my wife." Jim tried to rise but the doctor held him back.

"I want you to see her, too, Jim," Dr. Vender assured him. "And the fastest way for that to happen is for you to rest a bit longer and let me treat your wounds. Like Julia, you probably also have a concussion from the bullet that nearly took the top of your head off. And I had to dig deep to remove the bullet from your back. Your wounds would have killed most men. If you're not careful they might still kill you."

"You made your point, Doc," Jim replied. "Just patch me up so I can get outta here as quick as possible."

"That's exactly what I'm doing," Dr. Vender answered. He pulled back the sheets to expose Jim's back. He removed the bandages. "Your back wound is healing nicely," he said. "Much quicker than I expected. And there's no sign of infection."

Dr. Vender cleaned, redressed, and rebandaged the wound. He did the same for the deep bullet slash across Jim's scalp.

"The best thing for you right now is some more rest, Jim, and some food, broth and weak tea."

Dr. Vender waited for an argument from his recalcitrant patient, but, to his great surprise, the headstrong Ranger meekly agreed with his instructions.

"Whatever you say, Doc," Jim said, "as long as I can see Julia soon."

"I promise that you'll be able to visit her, at least briefly, in the next day or two. Now, do you have any more questions?"

"How long have I been here?"

"Five days. Does that matter so much?"

"It means those *hombres* have a five day head start on me."

"And they'll have several more before you can get out of that bed," Dr. Vender explained. "Besides, Captain Trumbull has several Rangers already working on finding those men. You know they want to track them down as badly as you do. They'll find them."

"You know anything about my horses, Doc, especially Sam?"

"Not really. I know the captain has a Ranger

guarding your ranch. I'm sure your horses are being well cared for."

"But Sam was hurt real bad. I tried to put him down, but my bullet missed when I passed out. I need to know about him, whether he's still alive or dead."

"I'll try and find out for you. Now that you're conscious, I'll let Captain Trumbull know he can see you in the morning."

"I'd like to see him right now."

"That's not possible. It's after ten o'clock at night. I promise I'll get the captain here as early as possible. Tell me you're not going to try anything foolish like getting out of that bed as soon as I leave the room."

"I reckon not." Jim lowered his head and sighed. "I can't do anything about it. You win for now, Doc."

"That's right," Dr. Vender agreed with a smile. "I'll have Jane bring in some broth and tea. I want you to take some laudanum for the pain and to help you get some more rest. I'll check on you again in the morning."

Chapter 6

"Jim, are you awake?"

"Sure am, Doc," the Ranger replied when Dr. Vender pushed his way through the door early the next morning.

"Good. Captain Trumbull's here to see you. I just wanted to be certain you weren't sleeping before I sent him in. Just remember I can't allow him to stay overly long. You still need your rest. I'll be back to check on you once the captain has finished his visit."

Dr. Vender disappeared and a few minutes later Jim's commanding officer, Captain Hank Trumbull, entered the room.

"Jim." The captain's normally booming voice was low and somber. "I'm sure sorry about what happened to you and your family. Doc Vender tells me Julia and Charlie are doing as well as can be expected. How about you?"

"Howdy, Cap'n. Good to see you," Jim replied, "Far as how I'm doin', I'm gettin' sick and tired of lyin' here on my belly and doin' nothin' while those *hombres* who shot up my boy and me and brutalized my wife are runnin' loose. You have any leads on 'em?"

"Not many, I'm afraid," Capt. Trumbull admitted.

The captain settled in a chair and pulled out his pipe and tobacco. "I've got every Ranger I can spare working on finding whoever did this," he explained, as he began filling his pipe. "But there's not much to go on. Nobody saw anyone leavin' your spread that day. And none of your horses have turned up anywhere, at least not yet."

"Speaking of my horses, how about Sam and Sizzle?" Jim asked.

"I've got Jeff Timmons out at your place takin' care of things," Trumbull answered. "Sizzle's fine. And Sam is still there. He's pretty well crippled up, but he's still eatin' and drinkin'. Seems like he's fightin' to live, at least maybe until he sees you again."

Capt. Trumbull paused, struck a match, and lit his pipe. He took a deep puff and exhaled a blue smoke ring toward the ceiling before he continued.

"You've got a tough decision about that horse facin' you, Jim."

"I'm aware of that," Jim replied, "But if there's any chance Sam can live without sufferin', I'm gonna give him that chance."

"I know what Sam means to you," Capt. Trumbull said, "but you have to do what's best for him."

"I know!" Jim snapped, more sharply than he'd intended. He sighed. "Sorry, Cap'n. It's just that . . ." Jim's voice broke.

"I understand, Jim."

Both men remained silent for a moment, the captain taking another long pull on his pipe.

"Jim," he finally asked, "What about you? You have any ideas about who might have done this?"

"Too many, I'm afraid," Jim answered. "But I'll tell you this, Cap'n. As soon as I'm out of this bed I'm gonna start trailin' 'em. And I'm not gonna quit that trail until every man responsible is dead. I ought to gut shoot 'em. No, better 'n that, I should strip 'em naked, coat 'em with honey, and stake 'em out on an anthill like the Comanche's would."

"Whoa, Lieutenant, rein in there," Capt. Trumbull protested. "I don't blame you for the way you feel. Lord knows I'd feel the same if this had happened to my family. But you can't take the law into your own hands."

Jim's voice quivered with anger as he replied. "Cap'n, if it'd just been me they'd gone after that would be one thing. But they nearly killed my wife and boy. Maybe they have, since Doc Vender's made no promises about Julia's and Charlie's recovery. They're gonna pay for that. Those *hombres* are dead men. I'll take em apart with my bare hands if I have to. Not one of 'em's gonna get away with what they did to my family. You can bet your hat on it."

"Jim, don't force me to do something I don't

41

want to. Don't make me take your badge."

"That's up to you, Cap'n. But if you take it I'll go after those *hombres* anyway. There's nothing you can say or do to change my mind."

The two Texas Rangers' gazes met, neither man willing to back down.

"Jim, maybe all this talk is for nothing," Capt. Trumbull finally said. "By the time you're able to ride again we might well have already found those men. And once you've had time to think things over you'll know that I'm right. Those men will be brought to justice. You have my word on that."

Before Jim could frame a reply, Dr. Vender stuck his head in the door.

"I'm sorry, but I have to end this visit," he said. "I've got to change Jim's and Charlie's bandages. Captain, you can visit Jim again tomorrow morning."

"All right," Capt. Trumbull said. "Jim, you think on what we talked about." He stood up and started for the door. "*Adios*, Ranger. I'll be back tomorrow."

"*Adios*, Cap'n," Jim answered, "and thanks."

After Capt. Trumbull left, Dr. Vender again treated Jim's wounds. Despite the Ranger's strong protests, the doctor still refused to let him out of bed to see his wife.

"Jim, if you take it easy for the rest of today and sleep well tonight, tomorrow you can see her," the physician assured him. "But be prepared for what you see. Julia is still severely bruised."

"I know how badly my wife was hurt, Doc. I saw the result of what those men did to her that day, remember?"

"I wasn't sure if you recalled anything from that morning."

"I remember every detail. Doc, I'm givin' it just one more day, then I'm gonna see my wife, no matter what you say."

"Hey, what's all that shoutin' in there? Is it safe for me to come in?" a voice called from just outside the room. Sheriff Tom Justus poked his head inside the door.

"You may come in, Sheriff, but only for a short visit," Dr. Vender answered.

"Jim, I thought you were bad hurt," the sheriff said smiling. "You'd never know it the way you were hollerin'. I thought you were fixin' to take the roof off Doc's place."

"Howdy, Tom. Good of you to stop by."

"Well, Maria and I had to see how y'all were doin'. She's sittin' with Julia right now. She'll stop by to see you before we leave, but she figured to let us talk first."

"Your wife always was a smart woman," Jim answered.

"Boy howdy, that's for certain," Justus agreed. "Jim, is there anything special we can do for you while you're laid up?"

"Not unless you can tell me who did this and where to find 'em."

"If I knew the answer to that, do you think I'd be here palaverin' with you?" Justus responded. "Me and half the men in this county'd be on their tails. Sure wish I had some idea, but I haven't got a clue. I suppose Capt. Trumbull's already told you the Rangers haven't had much luck either."

"He has," Jim said. "But once I'm up and outta here there's no place on earth those *hombres* can hide from me."

"I'm certain of that," Justus agreed. "And once you bring 'em in there ain't a jury in Texas that wouldn't convict those renegades and send them to the gallows."

"Who said I was gonna bring 'em in?"

Jim's voice was low and cold, his blue eyes glittering like chips of ice. Despite himself, Sheriff Justus shuddered. A chill went through him under the Ranger lieutenant's fierce gaze.

Dr. Vender broke in. "That's enough visiting for now. I still have to work on Charlie, and I can't do that while you're here, Tom," he said. "Why don't you give me half an hour or so, then you and Maria can stop back in and visit with Jim for a few more minutes?"

"That sounds like a fine idea," the sheriff agreed, relieved at Dr. Vender's timely appearance. "Jim, I'll join Maria and sit with Julia for

44

a bit, then we'll both see you before we leave. How's that?"

"That suits me just fine, Tom."

"Good. Then we'll be back shortly."

Once the sheriff and his wife left, Dr. Vender went to work on Charlie. He removed the bandages from the youngster's chest and back to clean the wounds. The Ranger kept the physician under his steady scrutiny while Vender worked on his son.

"Jim, you don't have to watch my every move."

"Sorry, Doc. It's just that I'm worried about my son."

"I know," the doctor replied. "So far I see no sign of infection. Charlie's wounds are beginning to heal. He is running a slight fever, but that's to be expected."

"So you're saying he'll be all right?"

"I'm saying there's a good chance of that. However, I'm making no promises. Charlie isn't out of the woods yet. He still has a long recovery ahead of him. But with the Lord's help he should be fine."

"I didn't mean to sound ungrateful," Jim answered, "I know you're doing everything you can for Charlie and Julia. And I sure appreciate that."

"I know you do, Jim. Look, I'm almost done here. Would you like me to send Tom and Maria back in?"

"If it's all the same to you, I'd just as soon get some more rest. I'm still kinda tired."

Dr. Vender scrutinized the Ranger. "Are you positive about that? I thought by now you'd be grateful for company. I expected you to be fighting to get out of that bed."

"Maybe tomorrow, Doc. Right now I'd just like to get some more shut-eye."

"I can't argue with you about that. In fact, I'm rather glad you want to sleep some more. Rest is nature's medicine." Dr. Vender pulled the covers back over Charlie. "I'll look in on you and your boy again tonight, Jim," he said.

"Sure, Doc. See you later."

Once Dr. Vender departed, Jim rolled onto his side and propped himself up on an elbow. He spoke softly as he gazed at Charlie, who lay motionless under the sheets, only his face visible.

"Charlie, I'm gonna be outta this bed in a couple of days. And as soon as I am, I'll be on the trail of the *hombres* who did this to you and your mom. And I won't stop until they're all dead. I promise you that, son."

Jim dropped back onto his pillow, rage tearing at his guts. Even his attempts at prayer for his wife and son came with great difficulty. Mercifully, he finally fell into a restless sleep.

Chapter 7

"Jim, I'm truly amazed at your recuperative powers," Dr. Vender noted the next morning. He had just finished his examination of the Ranger. "Your heartbeat is fine, your wounds are closing nicely, and there's no indication you're developing an infection. I'm pleased with your progress."

"So you're gonna let me outta here in a couple of days, right Doc?" Jim asked.

"Not quite so fast. We'll take one day at a time. I had counted on you being in that bed for at least a month, maybe, six weeks. But if you continue to do as well as you seem to be, you might be up and around in two or three weeks. But that will be only to get outside for some rest and fresh air. There will be no riding, and certainly no rangering. And, Jim, don't even think about arguing with me."

"I wasn't thinking about it, Doc," Jim answered. "I'm gonna lie here, take it easy, and follow doctor's orders."

"Jim, you have never done that for as long as I've known you. Why should I believe you are going to start now?"

"Because I want to be back to one hundred percent when I ride after those *hombres*!"

"I understand. But you'd best forget about those men and let Captain Trumbull take care of finding them. You won't be riding for at least two months."

"Want to bet a hat on that?" Jim grinned for the first time since he'd been shot.

Dr. Vender shook his head. "Not a chance, Jim Blawcyzk. I've known you too long to be foolish enough to take that bet. But I am going to give you some good news. Julia has improved a bit. She's still in a coma, but she's breathing more easily. I'll let you visit her after you've had some breakfast. Only for a short while though."

"Thanks, Doc. I sure appreciate it."

"I'm being a bit selfish," Dr. Vender admitted. "Letting you visit your wife will do the two of you some good. I believe it will help both of you heal more quickly. I'll have Jane bring in your breakfast now. Once you've finished eating you can see Julia. I had some clothes brought from your place. They are in the middle drawer of that chest next to your bed. Oh, your pistol's in there too, whenever you're ready for it."

After Jim rushed through a light breakfast, he threw on his shirt, jeans, and socks.

Dr. Vender smiled when he returned to find Jim sitting on the edge of his bed. "I should have known you'd be waiting for me. Just remember Julia won't know you're with her, or at least won't be able to respond. But as I said, your presence certainly can't hurt, and it may help."

"Let's go," Jim urged. He stood up too fast and the room started to spin. His first steps were faltering.

"Let me help you," Dr. Vender said. He took the Ranger by the elbow, steadying him.

Jim stopped short and took in a sharp breath when he entered Julia's room. Her appearance was far worse than he recalled. His wife's forehead was wrapped in a clean white bandage, another taped to her chin. Bruises, deep purple and brownish-yellow, still marred her face.

"Are you sure you're ready for this, Jim?" Dr. Vender questioned. "I did try to prepare you."

"I'm ready, Doc, and if you don't mind, I'd like to spend some time alone with Julia."

"Of course." Dr. Vender pulled a big gold turnip watch from his vest pocket and glanced at it. "I'll give you twenty minutes. And if you feel dizzy or nauseous, call me immediately."

"All right," Jim agreed. He eased into a hardback chair by his wife's side and wrapped his hand around hers. For several minutes he sat quietly at her side, holding her hand and fighting back tears. Finally he was able to contain his emotions sufficiently to whisper to her.

"Julia, I don't know if I can live without you. You've been the best part of me for all these years. And Charlie sure needs you too. Doc

Vender says Charlie's doing just fine. And he says you'll be just fine, too."

Jim hesitated before he continued.

"Julia, even though the doc says you'll recover, he also says it's gonna take some time. I might not be here when you wake up. I've got to get on the trail of the ranahans who did this to you. And every day I'm waitin' to get on their trail gives them more time to get away with what they did. I can't let that happen. So I'll be after 'em as soon as the doc says I can ride, maybe sooner. If I'm not here when you come to, please understand. I love you so much. I always will. And I know, with Doc Vender takin' care of you and the Lord's help, you and Charlie will be all right. And I'll come back to you as quick as I can. Once those *hombres* are in the ground I'll be home. And while I'm on the trail I'll make sure to keep in touch with Cap'n Trumbull so he can let me know how you're doin'."

Jim's voice trailed off. He sat there in silence, holding Julia's hand until Dr. Vender returned.

"Jim, I really hate to do this," said the doctor, "but it's time for you to get back to your own bed. You can't afford to overtax your system."

"I guess you're right," the Ranger conceded. "I am feelin' a bit groggy again."

Jim squeezed Julia's hand, then leaned over and kissed her. A slight smile spread across her face.

"Doc, did you see that?"

"I sure did, and that's a real good sign. The best one I've seen so far," the physician replied. "Tomorrow you'll be able to stay with Julia a bit longer."

Jim spent the rest of the morning sleeping, until his nap was interrupted by a soft tapping on his door. Jane Brady, Doctor Vender's nurse and assistant, poked her head into the room.

"Jim, are you awake?"

"I am now," he said. He rolled onto his back.

"Good. I have a couple of visitors for you."

The door swung open and Father Robert Biron, the pastor of the Blawcyzk's parish, St. Cecilia's Roman Catholic Church, stepped into Jim's room, along with Father Gary Koszmowski, his assistant.

"Father Biron! And Father Gary! I was wondering when you were gonna stop by," Jim exclaimed.

"Good morning, Jim," Father Biron said. "We already have been by several times to visit you and your family while you were still unconscious. In fact, since Doctor Vender indicated the seriousness of your conditions, we administered Extreme Unction to all of you. Hopefully, however, our prayers, and those of all your friends and everyone in the parish, will be answered and you, Julia, and Charlie will recover fully. You certainly seem to be doing just that. You're looking very well."

"Thanks, Father. I'm not feelin' all that bad, either. Just wish I could get outta this bed."

"Jim, you always were one of the most impatient men I've ever known." Father Koszmowski chuckled. "So I know you're well on the way to recovery if you're already trying to escape from Dr. Vender's care. I know it isn't easy, but try and remember it wouldn't do you any good to rush things. You'll be up and around before you know it."

"Maybe even before Doc Vender knows it." Jim laughed.

The priests and Jim spent almost three-quarters of an hour visiting. Finally, Father Biron got out of his chair.

"Jim, we have to make several more visits," he said. "We'll stop by on Thursday and bring Holy Communion for you. Is there anything else we can do for you?"

"Just one thing, Father," Jim answered. "I want to confess that I've killed a man, in fact several men."

Father Biron sighed. "We've had this discussion before. As we've said, the killings you have done in the line of your duties as a Texas Ranger are justified both in the sight of the Church and the sight of the Lord."

"This time will be different," Jim said. "You see, Father, as soon as I'm able to sit a saddle,

I'm goin' after the *hombres* who shot my boy and violated my wife. And I won't rest until every last one of 'em is dead. I'm not gonna give 'em the chance to surrender. I'll gun them down where they stand. They're gonna get the same chance they gave Julia and Charlie."

"Jim, I can't even begin to imagine what you are feeling. I won't insult you by trying to say that I do. But I do know that what you intend to do is wrong. You have every right to try and bring those men to justice, but you don't have the right to seek revenge, or to take the law into your own hands."

"You mean I should let those men to get away with what they did?"

Father Biron put his hand on Jim's shoulder. "You know that's not what I meant. Jim, if you exact revenge on those men, you'll be no better than them."

"Father Biron is right, Jim," Father Koszmowski added. "After all, 'Vengeance is Mine, sayeth the Lord.' "

Jim's blue eyes blazed with an unholy fury when he answered.

"Father Gary, vengeance may well be the Lord's, but I'm gonna be His right hand in meting out that vengeance. Those renegades won't only be facing the Lord's retribution, but the retribution of a Texas Ranger. And when I catch up with 'em, they'll be sorry the devil hadn't roped 'em in first, because by the time I'm done with 'em they'll wish they were in Hell. But they're gonna die real hard and painful before they get there."

Father Biron's eyes held a deep sadness, but also great sympathy as he responded to the soul-shattered Ranger's tirade.

"Jim, no one should have to go through what you and your family have suffered. But another wrong won't undo this injustice. Just hear me out." He raised his hand when Jim started to protest.

"You're hurting very deeply, both physically and to the depths of your soul. It's impossible for you to think clearly right now. Father Gary and I will be back on Thursday. I'd like to request you think about your intentions over the next two days. You also need to pray to the Lord for His guidance. I'm sure you will see Father Gary and I are correct, and once the anger you are feeling subsides you will realize that. And as soon as you do, then you will be able to begin your search for those men as a quest for justice, not reprisal. And you will be justified in that mission. Will you promise to do that?"

"The only promise I'm makin' is to see those *hombres* in the ground." Jim's anger had not receded.

"Will you at least try?" Father Koszmowski asked.

There was a moment of awkward silence before Jim answered the young priest.

"All right, I'll think about it, but nothing's gonna change my mind, or stop me from what I have to do."

"That's all we're asking for now," Father Biron said. "Now we really do have to leave. We'll pray you make the right decision, Jim."

The pastor blessed Jim, making the Sign of the Cross over the wounded Ranger.

Once the priests departed, Jim offered a prayer of thanks that Julia and Charlie were still alive, despite the bitterness gnawing at his guts. He tossed restlessly for quite some time before he finally fell into a fitful sleep.

Jim spent the next several days recuperating. His parish priests had again stopped by, still attempting to dissuade the Ranger from his vow to avenge the attack on his family. Their efforts only seemed to harden Jim's determination.

While Dr. Vender worked on Charlie one morning, the anxious Ranger questioned the physician.

"Doc, Charlie seemed sort of restless all night. His tossin' and turnin' kept me up until early this morning, before he finally settled down. Is he gettin' worse?"

"I don't believe so," Dr. Vender replied while he changed the bandage on Charlie's chest.

"His fever is a bit higher again, but that's not unexpected. With a bullet wound as severe as your son's, a body's temperature will fluctuate. In fact, I feel his restlessness is a positive sign. I believe Charlie will be regaining consciousness soon, at least for a short while. Again, that's to be expected during his recovery. He'll drift in and out for several days. But I finally think he has a good chance of surviving, although even after he regains consciousness he still won't be out of the woods by any means."

"That's the best news you've given me yet, Doc," Jim almost yelled.

Late that afternoon, Jim was half-asleep when he heard a soft murmur coming from the next bed.

"Charlie?" he called. "Charlie?"

"Dad is that you?" came a whispered response.

"It sure is, son," Jim answered.

"Where are we?"

"We're at Doc Vender's. I'd better call him now that you're awake."

"Where's Mom?"

"Your Mom's here too. She's sleeping in the next room. Now let me get the doc."

Jim got out of bed and went to the door.

"Doc! Doc Vender!"

"What is it, Jim?" the doctor answered from the front room.

"Charlie's awake!"

"I'll be there in a moment."

Jim could hear Dr. Vender's murmur as the physician explained to another patient he would return to her as quickly as possible. A minute later he was with the Ranger and his son. Jim settled back in his own bed while Dr. Vender went over to Charlie.

"Hello, Charlie." The doctor placed his hand on the boy's forehead. "I'm glad to see you're with us again, son. How are you feeling?"

"I'm kinda tired, Dr. Vender," Charlie answered. "And my chest is awful sore."

"I'm not surprised," Dr. Vender answered. "But at least your fever seems to be down. Charlie, do you remember what happened to you?"

"Sure. I got shot. I don't remember what happened after that, though."

Dr. Vender gave a soft chuckle. He took Charlie's wrist to check his heart rate. "I don't imagine you do. But that's why your chest is sore. I took a pretty large chunk of lead out of you. In fact, I saved it if you'd like to keep it. That bullet would have killed most grown men, let alone a youngster like you. You're one tough boy, Charlie Blawcyzk."

"You mean, tough like my dad?" Charlie asked.

"Yes, tough just like your dad." Dr. Vender laughed. He let go of the boy's wrist.

"Charlie, you seem to be doing fine. Since that's the case, I'm going to finish with my other patients. I'm sure you'd like to visit with your dad for a while. I'll return to change your bandages later."

"Okay, Doctor Vender."

"Jim, don't you wear him out."

"I won't, Doc," Jim assured him.

Once Dr. Vender departed, Jim swung his legs over the edge of his mattress to sit up. "Charlie, you gave me quite a scare," he said. "For a while there I thought I was going to lose you. Thank the Lord you're going to be all right."

"Dad, what about you? I know you got shot too. And what happened to Mom? Did those men hurt her?"

Jim hesitated before answering.

"I'll be fine. And yes, those men did hurt your Mom. That's why she's here. They didn't shoot her, but she was badly injured. It might take her a long while to recover."

"She's not gonna die, is she Dad?"

"Doc Vender says he's doing everything he can for her, and she should be fine," Jim answered. "But she does need us to pray for her."

"What about those men? Did the Rangers find them?"

"Not yet. But they won't get away. Soon as I'm a bit stronger, I'll be takin' the trail of those *hombres*. And I won't be back until I find 'em. So I'm gonna need you to get better quick so you can look after your Mom until I get back."

"I will, Dad. Count on me."

Charlie's voice was hushed, almost a whisper.

"Dad, I shot one of those men."

"You did what, Charlie?"

"I shot one of those men. When I heard gun-shots, I ran out of the barn. I saw you lyin' on the ground. I knew right then you'd been shot. Then I saw riders comin', so I grabbed your gun. I nailed one of 'em right in the stomach."

"So that's why my gun was in your hand. You shot a man off a gallopin' horse with one shot from a six-gun? That's some shootin', son."

"Thanks, Dad. I reckon it was as much luck as aim."

"Doesn't matter. At least you got one of 'em. Charlie, this is important. Do you think you killed that feller?"

"I dunno, Dad. I know I drilled him plumb center. He kinda sagged over his horse's neck, and then fell off. But that's when I must of got shot, because I don't remember anything after that. I'm sorry, Dad."

"There's no need to be sorry. You did what you could. I'm just sorry you had to shoot a man."

"I'm not, since he might've been the skunk who plugged you," Charlie answered. "When I saw you lyin' in the mud, I thought you were dead. I had to do somethin'. It did make me a bit sick to my stomach when I saw him get hit, though."

"You should always regret havin' to kill a

man," Jim gently chided. "But I can understand your feelin's."

"Why'd those men do this, Dad?"

"I don't know, Charlie. Probably lookin' to get even with me. When I catch up to 'em, I'll ask 'em for you."

"But why'd they hurt Mom?"

"For the same reason they hurt you. They knew that'd tear me up inside, and would hurt me more'n any bullet in my guts. Of course, they didn't plan on leavin' me alive either. I reckon they thought they'd finished me. They sure figured wrong, and they're gonna be sorry for that."

Jim paused for breath.

"Charlie, do you know how many of them there were?"

"I think there were six or seven of 'em."

"You didn't notice what any of 'em looked like, did you?"

"No. They were too far off. The man I shot was ridin' a roan. Couple or three of 'em were on bays. One of the bays had a star on its forehead. There was a blaze-faced sorrel, a stocking-footed chestnut, and a gray."

"Just like your ol' dad, notice the cayuses, eh, Charlie?" Jim laughed. "That's good. It'll help me track 'em down."

"I sure wish I could ride with you, Dad," Charlie said.

"And I'd like to have you sidin' me," Jim answered. "But you're still a bit too young, and like I said I need you to take care of your mom."

Jim glanced toward the door when it opened and Dr. Vender returned.

"I wasn't expectin' you back so fast, Doc," he said.

"I didn't have any patients who couldn't wait until tomorrow. I cancelled the rest of my appointments for the day so I could tend to you and Charlie," Dr. Vender explained. "I knew you'd keep talking with Charlie until I came back, and I don't want him to become exhausted. And Captain Trumbull is outside. If you don't mind him watching while I work on you two I'll bring him in."

"That's not a problem at all," Jim answered.

"Fine. We'll be right back."

Dr. Vender disappeared, returning a moment later with Captain Trumbull.

"Howdy, Jim. Howdy, Charlie," the captain boomed. "This is an unexpected surprise findin' you awake, son. That's certainly good news."

"Thanks, Captain Trumbull," Charlie replied.

"Cap'n, any word of those renegades?" Jim began.

"Just hold on a minute. You and the captain can talk while I change your bandages, Jim. Now flop over on your belly," Dr. Vender ordered.

"All right." Jim rolled onto his stomach, and

the doctor commenced removing the bandages from his back.

"Any news, Cap'n?" Jim asked.

Captain Trumbull filled his pipe and lit it. He took a puff before answering.

"Not much, I'm afraid. There hasn't been a sign of those men. We couldn't find much at your spread to help us identify who they might be, either. There's not a lot to go on."

"What about my horses? Ouch. Take it easy Doc, will you?" Jim protested, when Dr. Vender yanked a last stubborn length of bandage from the Ranger's back.

"I'm sorry, Jim."

"It's all right," Jim said.

"There hasn't been a sign of them," Capt. Trumbull answered. "We've checked with all the horse traders in the area, and of course we sent wires all over the state askin' anyone who might be offered broncs answerin' the description of your herd to contact us. But there's not much hope of that."

Charlie spoke up from his bed.

"Dad, all of our horses were stolen?"

"I'm afraid so, Charlie, except Sam and Sizzle," Jim answered. "Sam wouldn't let himself be taken, of course, but he was badly hurt fightin' those *hombres* off. And they did take Sizzle, but he got away somehow and came back home."

Charlie's voice trembled as he fought back tears.

"They even took Ted?"

Ted was Charlie's pet buckskin paint gelding. Jim had given him the gentle horse when Charlie was only a toddler, and Ted a yearling. Boy and horse had grown up together.

"Yes, they did. But I'll get him back for you. When I come back from runnin' down those outlaws I'll have Ted with me. You can bet your hat on it."

Captain Trumbull nearly choked on his pipe as he spluttered a protest.

"Wait a minute, Lieutenant. I thought we'd settled that. You're gonna stay right here and recuperate. Leave findin' those *hombres* to the rest of the Rangers. We want to find 'em as badly as you do. Smoky McCue will be back from Denton in a few days, and I've already sent for Jim Huggins. He'll be ridin' back from San Angelo any day now. I'm assigning them special to this case. You know Huggins is the best there is when it comes to turnin' up clues no one else can. He and Smoke will track down those renegades."

Jim started to rise from his bed in anger. "Cap'n . . ."

"Hold it right there, Jim," Dr. Vender ordered. "I can't change your bandages with you jumpin' around like that. Now just lie still until I'm done.

63

You and the captain can continue this argument once I'm finished."

"But," Jim began.

"No buts, son, get back on your belly. Ten minutes while I replace the bandages won't make a difference."

With a long sigh, Jim settled back on the bed.

A short while later Dr. Vender taped the last new bandage to the Ranger's back.

"There. I'm done. In a few more days, you'll be able to get outside for a bit and sit in the sunlight. That should make you feel a little better. Now you and the captain can talk while I take care of Charlie," Dr. Vender said.

Jim glared at Captain Trumbull.

"There's only one thing that will make me feel any better, and that's gettin' after the *hombres* who did this."

Capt. Trumbull took another pull on his pipe.

"And I ordered you to stay outta that search, Lieutenant. You know that. I can't say I know what you're feelin', but I can say with what happened to your wife and boy you're not thinkin' straight."

"You can't keep me from goin' after those renegades," Jim said. "There's nothing you can say or do that will stop me."

"Jim, you're too personally involved. I need men who can think objectively if we're to have any chance of finding our quarry."

"Will you two stop shouting at each other?" Vender interrupted, "I can't concentrate on my work with all your noise. Take an example from this boy here. He's staying perfectly quiet."

Dr. Vender had removed the old bandages from Charlie's chest and was cleaning out the boy's wound.

"I apologize, Doctor," Capt. Trumbull said. "We'll speak more softly. Jim, I hope you understand what I'm saying."

"Cap'n, you know I've never disobeyed your orders."

This time Capt. Trumbull did choke on his pipe. "What?"

"Well, maybe a time or two, but you have to let me go after that bunch. That's my boy lyin' in the next bed with a bullet hole in his chest and my wife who was beaten and . . ."

Jim stopped, not wanting Charlie to know the awful details of the attack on his mother.

"All the more reason you need to stay here with them," Capt. Trumbull answered.

"And what would happen if you took off before you were fully healed?" Dr. Vender put in. "You'd probably reopen your wounds, they'd get infected, and you'd die. That means those men would still escape and you wouldn't be around for your wife and son. What would that prove? Listen to Captain Trumbull. Your fellow Rangers will find those outlaws."

"There's another person in this room who should have a say," Capt. Trumbull added.

The Ranger captain turned to Jim's son. "Charlie, what do you think your dad should do?"

"Cap'n, that's not fair puttin' my boy on the spot like that," Jim protested.

"He should have as much say in this as you, Jim. Charlie, do you want to answer my question?"

"Sure, Captain Trumbull," Charlie replied. "My dad's the best Texas Ranger ever. He'll get those skunks that hurt my mom. I can take care of her while he's gone. My dad'll get my horse back, too."

"See, Cap'n," Jim said. "Even my boy knows what needs to be done. Thanks, Charlie."

"I should have guessed what Charlie's answer would be, knowin' how much he thinks of you," Capt. Trumbull grunted, "But that doesn't change a thing. Jim, if you try and go after those men, I'll take your badge. And if I need to I'll have you arrested. I mean that."

"All right, Cap'n, you win," Jim said. "Reckon that means I'm finished as a Ranger."

"That's not what I meant at all. There's still plenty of work for you once you're better. I can send you to a dozen trouble spots in Texas right now."

"I'll go along with whatever you say," Jim grudgingly answered.

"You'll see I'm right, Jim. Since that's settled, I've got to get back to Headquarters."

"Dad, shouldn't you tell Captain Trumbull about the man I shot?" Charlie asked.

"What? You shot one of those men?" Capt. Trumbull exclaimed.

"I sure did. I plugged him right in his belly," Charlie answered.

"Charlie told me he'd done that just before you came in, Cap'n," Jim explained. "I was gonna tell you but then we started arguin' and I didn't get around to it."

"I didn't treat anyone for an abdominal wound, that's for certain," Dr. Vender said.

"Of course not," Capt. Trumbull answered. "Those men wouldn't dare stop at any doctor around here. I'll send wires out immediately to see if any medico within twenty-five miles or so treated anyone who'd been gut-shot. I'll do the same with the undertakers, in case they handled anyone recently who'd died from a bullet wound."

"It would be highly unlikely for anyone with a .45 slug in his intestines to be able to ride very far," said Dr. Vender.

"If Charlie shot that *hombre* plumb center like he says then he's dead," Jim said. "His pards probably buried him someplace where the grave wouldn't be found that easy."

"You're probably right," Capt. Trumbull agreed, "but we have to be sure."

"Before you go, Charlie got a pretty good description of the horses those *hombres* rode, too." Jim added.

"That's good," Capt. Trumbull answered. "I can put that out also. I'll get right on it."

"And once Charlie's given you what you need you'll have to leave, Captain," Dr. Vender ordered. "The boy's already done too much. He only regained consciousness a couple of hours ago. He still needs plenty of rest."

He taped the last strip of bandage to Charlie's chest.

"I'm done here, Charlie. You've been a fine patient, not at all like your dad. Now you can tell the captain about those horses."

Charlie provided his description of the raiders' mounts.

"Good job, son. This might just help a lot," Capt. Trumbull praised Charlie.

"And now I have to insist you leave, Captain. I know Jim only too well. He'll keep you here half the day if I let him."

"All right," Capt. Trumbull said. "Jim, don't fret. We'll find those renegades, and when we do they'll be brought to justice. In the meantime you and your boy rest so you can both get back in the saddle as quick as possible. I'll be back to visit you the day after tomorrow."

"*Adios*, Cap'n."

"*Adios*, Jim, Charlie," Capt. Trumbull replied.

"And Charlie, keep your dad in line for me, will you?"

"You can count on me, Captain Trumbull."

Once the captain left, Dr. Vender gave his patients one last going over. "You're both doing fine," he said, "but I want the two of you to try and sleep some more. Charlie, I'm going to give you just a bit of laudanum to help ease your pain. Jim, I don't think you'll need any more at this point. I know you prefer not to take it anyway, and I don't want to chance your becoming addicted." Dr. Vender put the top on the bottle of laudanum. "I'll be back to look in on you later, and I'll have Jane bring a bit of supper for you then. In the meantime is there anything else you need?"

"Doctor Vender, when can I see my mom?" Charlie asked.

"Perhaps tomorrow if you feel up to it, Charlie. That's why you need to rest some more."

Charlie's eyes reflected his disappointment.

"Doc, there is one thing you can get for me," Jim asked.

"What's that?"

"I could use a pencil and some paper. I want to jot down a few notes."

"I'll send Jane right in with some."

As soon as Dr. Vender left the room, Charlie leaned up on his elbow and called out to his father. "Dad?"

"Yeah, Charlie?"

"You're not gonna listen to Captain Trumbull, are you? You're goin' after those men who shot me and hurt Mom, and stole my horse."

"That's right, Charlie. I couldn't live with myself if I didn't."

"Good. I knew you would, Dad. I want you to. I know Mom would want you to also. No matter what happens."

"Thanks, Charlie. Knowin' that makes my leavin' you and your mom behind while I go after those renegades a whole lot easier."

"How soon are you leaving?"

"Just before sunup, when I'm sure Dr. Vender will be asleep. I'll need to borrow his horse and buggy to get to our place. As soon as it's light enough, I'll search for any clues around our house then hit the trail. That'll give me a good start before Capt. Trumbull finds out I'm gone."

"Dad, I'm startin' to get sleepy again."

"That's the laudanum, plus you're still fightin' off the effects of that bullet," Jim pushed out of bed and stood at Charlie's side.

"Charlie, I just want to tell you how proud I am of you, son. And don't worry. I'll be comin' home soon as I can. But I won't be back until I've run down every one of the *hombres* who shot you."

"I know," Charlie murmured. As the drug took more effect, the boy looked at Jim's bullet-scarred upper torso and chuckled.

"Guess I'm gonna have a bullet mark on me just like you, Dad."

"Looks that way, Charlie." Jim forced a grin.

"Good luck, Dad. I'll pray for you, every day."

"Thanks, son."

Jim tousled Charlie's hair.

"I love you, Charlie."

There was no response. The laudanum had done its work, and Charlie was fast asleep.

Jim sat on the edge of his bed, taking pencil in hand. He smoothed a sheet of paper on the bed stand and wrote:

My dearest Julia,

I have never been able to find the right words to tell you how deeply I love you. Nothing will ever change how I feel about you. I want to be sure you know that, so I'm writing you this letter before I leave to do what I must do.

I have to find the men who tried to destroy our family and make sure they pay for what they did to you and Charlie. I couldn't face you if I didn't do everything I could to track them down. I know you'll understand that I have no choice.

Charlie is recovering fast and he's promised to help care for you until I return. You and he will be in my prayers every day. I am sure, with the Lord's help and Doctor Vender's care, you will soon be well. I will return to you as quickly as possible. Until then, I remain,

Your loving and devoted husband

Jim

Jim looked over his letter, folded it, and set it aside. He stretched out on his bed, prayed and lay staring at the ceiling until sleep finally claimed him.

About half an hour before the sun rose, Jim awakened. He slid into his clothes and boots and tucked his Colt into his waistband. As was his habit, he tousled Charlie's hair. He turned to leave, then turned back, leaned over, and kissed the sleeping boy's cheek.

"I love you, Charlie. Take care of your mom for me."

Jim slipped out of the room, closed the door, and crept into Julia's room. He placed his letter on the table by her bed and took her hand in his.

"Julia, I love you. Never doubt that, and never forget that," he whispered.

Jim fought back tears as he kissed Julia's lips. He sat alongside her for a few more moments and prayed for her recovery.

"Julia, I have to leave now," he finally said.

Without looking back, Jim got up, left the room, and quietly made his way from the house to the stable.

"Easy, Bess, easy. That's a good girl." Jim's soft tones and gentle touch soothed the doctor's chestnut mare. He soon had her in harness. Moments later, he held the mare at a slow walk as she pulled Dr. Vender's buggy out of the yard. Once they had cleared the edge of town, Jim pushed her into a fast trot.

Chapter 8

Just below the top of the rise overlooking his JB Bar Ranch, Jim pulled the mare to a halt. He climbed out of the buggy and turned the horse back toward town.

"I'm gonna leave you here, Bess, and walk the rest of the way. It wouldn't do for Jeff to see me usin' the doc's rig. You head back home, girl."

Jim gave the mare a gentle slap on the rump. She'd taken a sleeping Dr. Vender home many times after he'd been up most of a night treating a severely ill patient or delivering a baby. Bess would be standing at her stall door within an hour.

Jim stood for a moment on the top of the rise to gaze down at the JB Bar looking peaceful in its tranquil little valley. The ranches appearance was softened by the early morning mist, and smoke curled from the chimney. Evidently Jeff Timmons was cooking his breakfast. The bucolic scene belied any evidence of the recent violence. The only indication of something amiss was the lack of horses in the pastures and corrals. But to Jim's great relief, Sam and Sizzle were still there, sharing a corral. Jeff Timmons' buckskin, Socks, was in the adjoining corral. The horses were munching their morning hay.

Jim whistled and both of his horses jerked up their heads, ears pricked forward at the familiar sound. The geldings spotted him as he started down the hill and trotted up to the fence, whinnying a greeting. Jim hurried to the corral and ducked under the rails.

"Whoa, easy there! Oof!"

Jim grunted as Sam buried his muzzle in his belly, while Sizzle nuzzled at Jim's neck, both horses nickering a welcome. Jim scratched their ears and laughed.

"How you boys doin'? Let me take a look at you."

Jim examined both paints. Sizzle was in fine shape, the raw scrapes on his neck almost completely healed.

"You look just fine, Siz," Jim said before turning to Sam. "Ol' pardner, I'm sure glad my bullet missed, I never thought I'd see you trottin' around again."

Covered with thick scabs, Sam's bullet wounds were healing well. Jim ran his hands down Sam's left foreleg, stopping just above the ankle. He carefully felt the large lump apparent there. Sam flinched when Jim pressed on the swollen tissue.

"I'm sorry, but I need to see you move out a bit, pal," Jim told the horse. He slapped Sam gently on the shoulder. The gelding snorted and trotted away, limping on that left leg. He turned and trotted back to Jim. Sam dropped his nose to

Jim's hip pocket, begging for his customary treat.

"Oh no you don't," Jim said laughing. "I'll get some peppermints for you in a while. They're in the house."

Jim once again ran his hands over Sam's left leg. "Sam, I'm not gonna have to put you down, thank the Good Lord." He stroked Sam's neck. "But your days of helpin' me run down renegades and Comanche are over. That tendon's never gonna be the same. Looks like you'll spend the rest of your life bein' lazy, doin' nothing but eatin' grass and gettin' fat. I know you might not be happy about that, and I'm sure gonna miss havin' you under me, but you deserve the rest, ol' pard. And I wish I could spend some time with you before I leave, but I've got to get movin'."

Jim turned back to Sizzle. "Soon as I gather up what I need, you and I are gonna hit the trail. And we won't be comin' back for a while, not until we run down the renegades who hurt you and Sam. I'd purely like to bring a couple of those *hombres* back for Sam to chomp on. Anyway, Siz, I guess you're gonna have to be a Ranger mount after all. Your career's startin' a bit sooner than I'd planned, but I know you'll give me your best."

Jim gave both horses a final pat on their muzzles, then went to the house. He opened the front door and stepped into the kitchen.

Jeff Timmons was at the stove. He whirled at the sound of footsteps behind him, yanking his Colt from its holster.

"Hey! Careful, Jeff!" Jim shouted raising his hands shoulder high as Timmons leveled his six-gun at Jim's stomach. "It's me, Jim. I own this place, remember?"

"Jim!" Jeff put up his gun. "Sure didn't expect to see you. I thought you were still at the doc's. And you should know better'n to sneak up on a man like that."

Jim lowered his hands.

"I reckon you're right. I just didn't think about it, bein' back home and all."

"It's good to see you," Jeff said. "But what're you doin' here? Last I'd heard you were gonna be laid up for at least a couple more weeks."

"Doc Vender said I could recuperate just as well here as at his place, so he let me go," Jim responded.

"That is good news. What's the word on Julia and Charlie?"

"Charlie seems to be doin' right well. He should be fine. The doc says Julia's gonna be fine too, but she's still in a coma."

"I'll keep prayin' for them," Jeff promised.

"I appreciate that."

"Jim, I've got breakfast just about ready. You want some grub?"

"Sure, sounds good."

Jim glanced around the kitchen, which was spotlessly clean. Everything was back in place, the broken china gone. There was not a sign of the mess left by the attack on his wife.

"Looks like you did a bang up job cleanin' around here, Jeff. And my horses look like they're healing up right nicely too. I surely appreciate what you've done. I'm kinda surprised Sam let you near him."

"Thanks. It did take a while before Sam would trust me enough to even approach him. Far as the house, I couldn't leave it like it was. Only thing I wish is there'd been some clue left behind as to who did this. I went through everything with a fine toothed comb to make sure there wasn't somethin' we could have used." Jeff thumbed back his hat and ran his fingers through his sandy hair. "I found nothin'."

"Not much we can do about that." Jim shrugged. "Jeff, where'd you put my gunbelt and Stetson?"

"There wasn't much left of your hat. That bullet you took went clean through it. Plus it was blood and mud soaked, so sittin' in the sun for hours it shrank real bad. You'll need a new one. Far as your gunbelt, it's on the chest in your bedroom. Your Winchester's there too. While I've been watchin' your spread, I had time to replace the stock for you. That rifle's good as new."

"I'm grateful for that," Jim said. "That gun's been with me for quite a while."

"Least I could do," Jeff answered. He lifted the lid off the coffeepot. "Coffee's ready, and the bacon's just about done."

"That's fine. Listen, I'm gonna get my gunbelt. I'll be right back for that chuck."

"It'll be waitin' for you."

Jim disappeared into his bedroom. He took his gunbelt from the chest and buckled it on, sliding his Peacemaker into the holster on his left hip. He grabbed some spare clothes from a drawer and laid them on the bed. That done, he placed his Winchester alongside the clothes.

"I'm ready to dish everything out," Jeff said when Jim returned to the kitchen.

"I'm afraid I don't have time to eat," Jim answered. "Drop your gun and get your hands up, Jeff."

Jeff turned from the stove to see Jim, Colt in hand. The Peacemaker was leveled at Jeff's belt buckle.

"Jim? What is this?" Jeff's brown eyes were wide with disbelief as he stared down the barrel of the gun aimed straight at his gut.

"I said, unbuckle your gunbelt and drop your gun. The knife too. Then get your hands up. I won't ask you again."

Jim thumbed back the hammer of his Peacemaker.

"Guess I've got no choice."

Jeff unbuckled his gunbelt, let it fall, and lifted his hands over his head.

"You gonna tell me what this is all about?"

"Cap'n Trumbull ordered me not to go after the men who attacked me and my family. I can't take those orders," Jim explained. "I'm headin' out after 'em right now."

"You lied to me Jim. You weren't supposed to leave the doc's yet, were you?"

"Right smart guess," Jim answered. "Now lie down on your belly."

His gun still aimed at the young Ranger, Jim opened a drawer and removed a length of clothesline.

"Jim, there's no need for this," Jeff protested.

"Just get on your belly. Hands behind your back."

Jeff stretched out on the floor and Jim began to tie his hands together.

"Jim, I wouldn't stop you from goin' after those *hombres*," Jeff said. "In fact, I agree with you. You should go after 'em. I'd like to ride with you."

"I can't take the chance you're tellin' the truth," Jim answered. "Besides, this way you won't get into trouble with Cap'n Trumbull. You can tell him I got the drop on you and hogtied you."

Jim finished tying Jeff's wrists, and then he wrapped a rope around the young Ranger's ankles.

"I'm not tyin' you too tight. You'll be able to work yourself free in an hour or so," Jim said. "That'll give me enough time for the head start I need. And there's no one around to hear you shout, so I won't gag you."

"Jim, you're makin' a big mistake," Jeff said.

"Maybe so, but I have to do this." Jim checked Jeff's bonds one last time. "Jeff, you've been a good pard the times we've ridden together. I sure hope we can again someday. I'm real sorry I have to leave you like this, but I don't have any choice."

"I reckon I understand, Jim. I still think you're makin' a mistake, but I won't hurry and tell the captain about this. It might take me a few hours to get myself untied. Maybe even all night." Jeff grinned. "Good luck."

"I appreciate that, pard. Oh, and thanks for not puttin' up a fight. You know I never would've plugged you."

Jim started back toward the bedroom to retrieve his clothes and Winchester. He stopped short at the sound of approaching hoof beats and glanced out the window to see Dan Huggins tying his blue roan to the rail.

"Doggone it! I should've known there'd be a man along to relieve Timmons," Jim muttered.

Dan Huggins stepped through the kitchen door. He had just enough time for a glimpse of Jeff lying tied up on the floor before Jim sank his fist deep into the young Ranger's belly. Dan grunted as all the air was driven from his lungs. He folded, and Jim smashed a second blow to the point of Dan's chin, straightening him. Dan never knew what hit him. He stood for a moment, eyes glazing, and toppled forward. Jim bent to catch him at the waist, letting the stunned Ranger fall across his shoulder. He carried him into the living room and dropped him face-up on the couch.

"Looks like you'll be out for at least a couple of hours. Sorry, Dan," Jim spoke to the unconscious Ranger. "Sure hope your dad'll forgive me for doin' this to his boy."

Jim had ridden with Dan's Ranger father, Sergeant Jim Huggins, on many assignments. Huggins had saved Jim's life on at least one occasion.

Jim went back to the bedroom to pick up his spare clothes and his rifle. Returning to the kitchen he gulped a quick mug full of strong black coffee, then wrapped most of the breakfast Jeff had cooked in a kitchen towel. He also took a can down from a shelf, emptying its contents, peppermints, into his hip pocket. He checked the fire in the stove to make sure it was banked, so it would not overheat and set the kitchen ablaze.

"Jeff, I'm leavin' some grub for you and Dan," he told Timmons. "It'll still be warm by the time you get yourself untied and Dan wakes up.

I'm gonna turn your horse and Dan's out in the pasture with Sam."

"I can't change your mind?"

"Not a chance. I'm gonna catch up to those *hombres*, and they're gonna die with a bellyful of my lead in 'em. Bet a hat on it."

"Then all I can say is be careful, Jim, and *vaya con Dios.*"

"*Gracias*, Jeff. *Adios.*"

Jim dropped his spare clothes, supplies, and rifle on the porch. He untied Blaze, Dan's blue roan, and led him to the JB Bar's first pasture. He stripped the gear from the horse, dropped it to the ground, and gave him a gentle slap on the rump. Blaze snorted and trotted off a short distance. He dropped his nose to the thick grass and began to graze.

Jim repeated his actions with Socks, Jeff's stocking-legged buckskin. Once Jeff's gelding had joined Blaze, Jim retrieved his gear from the porch, and headed for the barn. He stuffed his clothes and supplies in his saddlebags and shoved the Winchester into its saddle scabbard. That done, he pulled the bloody shirt and Stetson from their hiding place and took the scrap of fabric and strands of hair he'd pried from Julia's hand out of his pocket. He rolled them carefully in a piece of oilcloth and slid them into a saddlebag. He tied his bedroll on the saddle's cantle.

Jim carried his saddle, saddle blanket and

bridle to the corral where Sizzle and Sam stood waiting. He slipped both horses a peppermint before saddling and bridling Sizzle. Sam watched curiously, nickering softly while Jim readied the other mount.

"Sam, I sure hate to leave you behind." Jim's eyes grew moist as he stroked the paint's nose, remembering all the trails they'd ridden together. "But I have a feelin' you know it's high time you rested and took it easy for a spell."

Sam nickered, and buried his muzzle in Jim's belly. Jim grunted.

"Can't say I'm gonna miss that little trick of yours, pard. Aw heck, yes I will, you ornery ol' bronc. Even though it's hard on my guts when you pull that stunt, bud."

Jim wrapped his arms around Sam's neck and buried his face in the paint's thick mane. Man and horse stood motionless for several minutes. Finally, Jim stepped back.

"Sam, I've really got to get movin'," Jim said. "You can take care of yourself until I come home again, that's for certain. There's plenty of grass and water for you. Charlie will be home to look after you before too long, and here are enough peppermints to hold you for a month."

Jim emptied his hip pocket, letting Sam munch an entire mound of candies. When the gelding had finished, Jim led him to the pasture, then turned him loose. Sam hesitated for just a moment, nickered, and then trotted off to join Socks and Blaze.

Jim's eyes were still moist as he fastened the pasture gate. By the time he reached Sizzle, his cheeks were tear-stained. He checked his cinches one last time, slipped the horse one peppermint he'd saved, and climbed into the saddle. "Let's go, Siz," he said, his voice still husky with emotion.

He heeled the tall gelding into a lope. When they started off, Sam lifted his head and let out a long, piercing whinny.

Chapter 9

Jim hadn't yet passed the west boundary of his ranch when he reined Sizzle to a halt and dropped from the saddle. He studied the set of tracks approaching his ranch. Even though it had twice rained hard since the attack, the hoof prints of the outlaws' horses were still visible in the soft soil.

"One thing that fools a lotta folks," Jim said to Sizzle, "is that rain doesn't wash out tracks as easy as most people think. It's plain to see there were eight riders in that bunch. Since Charlie claims he did in one of 'em, that means we're lookin' for seven men."

Jim climbed back into his saddle. He walked Sizzle in ever-widening circles until he found the sign he was seeking. The hoof prints of bunched, fast-driven horses led to the northwest.

"Here's where those rustlers drove the rest of your friends off, Siz. They'll have covered their tracks before goin' far, so these prints aren't much help. Now all we've gotta do is figure out where they headed. And that could be anywhere from here to New Mexico or anyplace in between. I've got no idea where those sidewinders might've gone to get rid of those horses. But I know an *hombre* who will. I'd bet my hat on it. Let's move, pardner."

Jim heeled the long-legged paint into a ground-covering lope. Sizzle's lengthy strides ate up the miles as the Ranger pushed him steadily westward. The only times he slowed the gelding were to check loose soil that might have marked a freshly-dug grave.

It was mid-afternoon when Jim rode into the town of Dripping Springs. Slowing the paint to a trot as they headed down the main street, Jim began glancing around. He'd been in this town quite often and knew every landmark by heart. Jim pulled Sizzle to a halt outside a complex of large, well-shaded corrals and a huge barn. A good number of fine looking horses lazed in the corrals, and the doors of the barn were open to let fresh air into the stalls. "Joseph Walier, Horse Trader," was emblazoned on the front of the stable in bold red letters. Underneath that smaller red letters proclaimed, "Horses, Wagons, And Carriages Bought, Sold, And Traded."

Jim swung out of his saddle and led his weary horse to a trough just outside the barn door. After the thirsty gelding sucked up a short drink, Jim tied him to a rail. He stepped into the stable and called for the proprietor.

"Joe! Joe Walier! Where the heck are you? I need to talk to you, and I'm in a hurry!"

In answer to the Ranger's shout, the stable

owner emerged from his office. Joe Walier had started his horse trading business in the small north Texas town of Keene, then expanded and moved it to Dripping Springs. He was tall and thin, his gray hair neatly combed under the light colored Stetson he wore. Besides his rather distinguished appearance, Walier had one trait which set him apart from most of the others in his business. Walier was scrupulously honest. He'd never cheated a man in a horse trade.

"That's gotta be Jim Blawcyzk doin' all that hollerin'. You're the last man I expected to darken my door, but I'm sure glad to see you," Walier grinned. "What brings you by, Lieutenant?" He took Jim's hand with a solid grip. "Where the heck is your hat?"

"Howdy, Joe. To answer your second question, my hat sorta got shot up. I'll pick up a new one first chance I get. As far as what brings me to Dripping Springs, this isn't exactly a social call."

"I had a feeling it wasn't. In fact, I've got a pretty good guess why you're here," Walier answered. He glanced out the door to see Sizzle tied to the rail.

"Jim! Is that your cayuse tied there? Lemme take a look at him. What happened to that cantankerous Sam horse of yours? You're not tellin' me you're ridin' another bronc?"

Walier walked over to Sizzle. He ran a hand

88

down the paint's shoulder. Sizzle nuzzled the horse dealer's face.

"That's one of the reasons I'm here," Jim answered. "And this is Sizzle."

With an experienced eye, Walier studied the horse, walking around the gelding and examining him from all angles.

"Well, he's a fine lookin' animal," he praised. "Young one, too. I can't see a thing wrong with him. Lot better personality than Sam, too. In fact, he seems like a downright friendly cuss. At least he didn't try and take my head off. You want to sell him?"

"Not a chance. As to what happened to Sam, he's crippled up. Tendon. Got shot a couple of times, too."

"I'd heard about what happened at your place. Couple of Rangers came by a few days afterwards to ask me some questions. I'm afraid I wasn't much help to 'em. They never mentioned Sam, so I didn't know he'd been hurt so bad. I know how much store you set by him. Forgive my bad manners, Jim. I was so surprised to see you I plumb forgot to ask about your family. How are Julia and Charlie?"

"Charlie's doin' pretty well. He should be fine, the doc tells me. But Julia's still in a coma. Doc says she should come out of it, but he's not sure how much damage those *hombres* might've done."

"I'm real sorry to hear that. I'm sure the Good Lord'll see to it that she recovers. And I'll keep her in my prayers."

"I appreciate that, Joe. And I'm gonna find the men who did all this. But I need your help."

"I'll do anything I can. Tell you what. Why don't you bring your horse, Sizzle, was it?"

"That's right, Sizzle."

"Bring Sizzle inside, take your gear off him, and put him in that fourth stall on the right. I'll grain and water him. While he's eatin' I'll put on some coffee. You look like you could use some. I've got some apple pie in the office too. We'll chow down and I'll answer whatever questions you might have."

Sizzle was soon settled in a stall, Jim and Walier seated in the hostler's office, working on pie and coffee.

"Jim, what'd you want to ask me?" Walier queried. He took another forkful of pie.

"You know just about every place where a man'd go to sell off stolen horses," Jim said. "All my broncs except for Sam were run off by the renegades who attacked my place. They did try to take Sam, but he fought 'em off. They even took Sizzle, but he broke free somehow and came home. I figure if anyone can tell me where my horses might be you can, Joe. Even though you say you weren't much help to those other Rangers."

"Jim, I would've provided those boys any information I had, you know that," Walier said. "I just didn't have anything to give them."

"I know, but you must've heard somethin'."

"I have since. There's word of a new bunch that specializes in stealing horses. From what I hear tell, they have a place over in Blanco County. They run the stolen stock in there, keep 'em hidden for a spell until things cool down a mite, then rework the brands and sell the broncs."

"Blanco's a lot of territory to cover," Jim said as he took another swallow of coffee.

"I know that. But the men you're lookin' for supposedly hole up somewhere along the Pedernales River, close to the falls. Not all that far from Johnson Settlement, in fact."

Jim set down his mug and rose to his feet. "Then that's where I'm headed. *Gracias*, Joe."

"You sure you don't want to spend the night and start out fresh in the mornin'?" Walier asked.

"Not a chance. Those *hombres* have already had too much time to get away," Jim answered. "I can put quite a few more miles behind me before sundown. Reckon I'll be ridin'."

The Ranger retrieved Sizzle from his stall, saddled and bridled him and climbed into the saddle.

"Joe, I appreciate your help," he said. "If anyone asks, I'd also be obliged if you don't let them know where I'm headed."

"What if any of your fellow Rangers come by again?"

"Especially if any Rangers stop by lookin' for me."

"I get your meanin', Jim. Far as I'm concerned I never saw you."

"Thanks, Joe. *Adios.*"

"You be careful, Jim. And *vaya con Dios.*"

Jim pointed Sizzle's nose westward once again. As soon as they cleared the outskirts of Dripping Springs, he heeled the paint into a lope.

Captain Hank Trumbull glared at the two men facing him. His voice reverberated throughout the corridors of Ranger Headquarters. Jeff Timmons was anxiously puffing on a quirly, while Dan Huggins stared down at the Stetson he twisted in his hands.

"Timmons, what in blue blazes do you mean Jim Blawcyzk got the drop on you? He was supposed to still be in bed at Doc Vender's place in San Leanna. The doc sent word a short while ago Jim disappeared sometime during the night. Turned out he stole the doc's horse and buggy. Doc Vender didn't even know Jim or his rig were gone until he went to feed his horse and found her hitched to the buggy and nosin' the stall door. And now you tell me Jim's off chasin' those renegades! I had you watchin' his spread in case he pulled a fool stunt like this, just as much as keepin' a lookout for anyone up to no good who might come snoopin' around. How'd you let this happen?"

"I'm sorry, Cap'n," Jeff said. "When the lieutenant showed up and said he'd been sent home by his doctor, I had no reason not to believe him. I sure never expected him to pull a gun on me."

"So you just let him stick a Colt in your belly."

"Hate to admit it, but that's about the size of it," Jeff confessed.

"What about you, Huggins?" Capt. Trumbull demanded.

"I dunno, Cap'n." Dan kept his eyes down. "I never even saw the lieutenant. I only caught a glimpse of Jeff lyin' tied up, and then somebody socked me real hard in my gut. I've never been hit in my belly that hard before, ever. That's the last thing I remember until Jeff dumped a bucket of water over my face. I can't even say for sure it was Jim who hit me."

"I suppose you're gonna tell me that lump on your jaw is a love tap from one of the gals at the Silver Star," Capt. Trumbull said in disgust.

Jeff chuckled, but quickly shut up at a glance from the captain.

Dan rubbed the huge bruise on his chin, flinching at the pain. "No, Cap'n, it sure wasn't from one of those gals. But whoever hit me left me with one heckuva bellyache and a real sore jaw."

"Well, thanks to you two, Jim Blawcyzk's on the loose and ridin' on a vendetta for those dirty sons who attacked his family," Capt Trumbull said. "And none of us have the faintest idea where to start lookin' for him."

"At least he's not ridin' that Sam horse of his," Jeff said. "Not havin' that cantankerous cayuse between his legs might slow Jim down some. A new horse is bound to take some trainin'. And it won't be used to hard travelin'."

"Have you forgotten Jim Blawcyzk's the best man with a horse on the entire force, probably in the entire State of Texas?" Capt. Trumbull looked like he was about to bust a gut. "A new mount isn't gonna bother him."

"What're we gonna do then?" Dan asked.

Capt. Trumbull's anger finally reached the boiling point.

"I don't know what I'm gonna do. I do know that both of you are confined to the barracks for two weeks. You're two of the poorest excuses for lawmen ever to pin on a Ranger badge!"

"Whoa, what's all the bellerin' in here? They can hear you clear down to the Capitol buildin', Cap'n."

Smoky McCue grinned as he stepped into Trumbull's office.

"McCue! Where have you been? You were supposed to be back yesterday!" Trumbull yelled.

"I did get back last evenin', late. Spent the night at home with my wife. I haven't seen Cindy Lou in a month of Sundays. And beggin' your pardon, Cap'n, but she's a heckuva lot better lookin' than you. And a whole lot more fun to spend the night with."

Smoky took the makings from his vest pocket and began rolling a cigarette.

"That's enough of your sass, Corporal. Jim Blawcyzk's defied my orders. He's on a vengeance trail. No thanks to these two!"

"Don't be too hard on these boys, Cap'n. Once Jim sets his mind to somethin', nobody's gonna stop him. You know that. Thing to do now is figure out what we're gonna do next."

"We're not gonna do anything," Trumbull answered. "You're gonna find Jim Blawcyzk and bring him back here. You're probably the only man in the Texas Rangers who can track him down. Well, you and Jim Huggins. I sent for him too, but got word he was shot up. He's on his way home to recuperate. Yes, he'll be fine," Trumbull anticipated Smoky's question, "Otherwise Dan wouldn't be here. But he will be laid up for a couple of weeks."

"If Jim Blawcyzk doesn't want to be found, I won't have much chance of catchin' up to him," Smoky pointed out.

"Maybe so, but you've ridden with Jim more than any of us. You and he've been pards for years. You know how he thinks. If anyone can find him, it's you, Corporal."

Trumbull's voice softened as he continued. "Smoky, you know how much I think of Jim. He's almost like a son to me. That's why I want to find him, before he gets himself killed. Doc Vender says Jim's still bad hurt, so if he tries to take on that bunch by himself he'll wind up with a gutful of lead. Or worse, he's liable to do something really stupid, like gunnin' those *hombres* down in cold blood. Then he'd be a killer just like them. I'd hate to see him swingin' from a rope."

"I doubt any jury in Texas'd convict him," Smoky said.

"Probably not," Capt. Trumbull agreed, "But we're still duty-bound to bring him in. And that means quite a few men might die in the attempt, since most likely Jim'd go down shootin'. The way he was actin' I doubt he'd surrender. He's half crazed with anger."

"Lt. Blawcyzk wouldn't shoot another Ranger," Dan protested. "And I'm not sure how many of us would try'n plug him."

"We can't take that chance," Capt. Trumbull answered.

"The captain's right, Dan," Smoky agreed. "Soon as he fills me in on everything, I'll be ridin'." He took a long drag on his quirly. "Captain, how's Jim's wife and boy doin'? I won't have time to visit them like I'd planned."

96

"That's another reason you need to find Jim as soon as possible. Julia's still unconscious, which he knows. But he thinks Charlie's on the mend. When the doc sent word that Jim had taken off, he also said Charlie took a sudden turn for the worse this mornin'. Blood poisoning's set in. And Jim doesn't know that."

"That's not good news," said Smoky. "Cap'n, do you have any idea where I should start?"

"I haven't got much of one. There hasn't even been a sign of Jim's rustled horses."

"Well, I know you won't believe this, but that does give me a place to begin. Jim'll head over to Dripping Springs and talk to Joe Walier. Joe'll have some idea about who might have stolen those broncs."

"I had Toby Jones and Rowdy McCandless talk to Walier. He claimed he didn't know a thing."

"Maybe he didn't, then, but he does by now. As Jim would say, I'd bet a hat on that."

"You want us to ride with you, Smoke?" Jeff asked.

"No. If I'm gonna have any chance of catchin' up to Jim, I'd best ride alone," Smoky replied.

"Besides, don't forget you two are confined to quarters for two weeks," Capt. Trumbull reminded Jeff and Dan.

"Cap'n, that's not fair," Smoky broke in. "They couldn't have known what Jim was up to."

"Maybe you're right, but they still shouldn't

have let him fool the both of 'em." Capt. Trumbull rubbed a gnarled hand down his face. "But since you're stickin' up for 'em, I figure I can cut the confinement to a week. Not a word or it goes right back to two," he warned before the others could object.

"Then that's settled," Smoky said. "Cap'n, tell me what I need to know."

Capt. Trumbull spent the next half hour going over everything that had happened from the day of the raid on the JB Bar to Jim's fleeing Dr. Vender's. Once he had finished, Smoky headed outside, climbed in the saddle of his steeldust, backed the horse away from the rail, and loped down Congress Avenue. Ten minutes later he reached the city limits and pushed Soot into a dead run.

Chapter 10

The approach of dusk found Jim still quite a distance from his destination, the falls and breaks of the Pedernales River. He was feeling the effects of his wounds and the days of inactivity. Every muscle in his body ached, and a deep weariness was settling in his bones.

"Siz, I guess it's about time to find a place to spend the night," Jim told his horse. "We've covered a lot of ground today, and I'm feelin' tired. 'Sides, it'll be dark soon, and we won't be able to do any searchin' tonight. I don't want to chance stumblin' onto someone and not bein' ready for 'em."

No sooner had Jim begun scanning the countryside for a suitable campsite when several shots rang out some distance ahead. Jim pressed his heels into Sizzle's ribs. The big gelding leaped forward in a dead run. Jim reined him in just before they reached the mesquite *bosque* from which the shots had come. He dropped from the saddle and lifted his Colt.

"We've got to go in slow and easy," he warned Sizzle, with a soft pat to his muzzle. "So you keep quiet, bud. Stay put until I call you."

Jim led Sizzle to the thicket and looped his horse's reins loosely around a thick branch.

Sizzle would be able to jerk free and come at his rider's whistle. The paint fell to munching on the mesquite pods.

Jim spied the faint glow of a campfire. He worked his way to the edge of the firelight. Alongside the fire was a peddler's wagon, its team of mules unhitched and hobbled for the night. A scraggly-bearded gunman had his pistol leveled at the wagon's owner, while a second man ransacked the conveyance.

"Texas Ranger! Don't move!"

Jim's voice cut through the still air like the crack of a whip.

The first gunman shifted his six-gun away from the trader and sent a wild shot in the direction of Jim's voice. Jim fired twice in return, both of his slugs tearing into the outlaw's stomach. The man dropped his gun, clamped both hands to his middle, spun and collapsed.

The second robber twisted around on the wagon seat. He fired blindly, three times; the slugs shattering brush over Jim's head. Jim fired once. His bullet slammed into the man's chest, blasting him off the wagon. The holdup man hit the ground hard and lay still.

"Don't move, Mister!" Jim ordered the peddler.

"I'm not twitchin' a muscle," the man called back.

Colt still at the ready, Jim stepped into the circle of firelight. He walked up to the first gunman and, with the toe of his boot, rolled him onto his back. The stomach-shot renegade let out one wracking cough, then his breathing ceased.

Jim moved over to the other robber. His bullet had pierced the man's heart, stopping in his spine. He died before he hit the dirt.

Jim punched the empties from his Colt and reloaded. He shoved the gun back in its holster.

"I'm sure glad to see you, Mister," the peddler declared. He was a stocky man somewhere on the north side of fifty. He took out a handkerchief to wipe sweat from his forehead.

"I figured I was a goner. Those bandits would've killed me once they'd taken what they wanted."

"It's Ranger, mister, Ranger Lieutenant Jim Blawcyzk. And it's likely they would've shot you," Jim said. "But they won't bother anyone else."

"Well, I appreciate your handlin' them, Ranger. Saved my bacon. I'm O'Neil St. Onge. You recognize either of those men?"

"Yep." Jim nudged the body of the first outlaw with his boot.

"This here's Riley Buxton. He was wanted for robbery and assault. The Rangers have been lookin' for him for quite a spell. And his pardner's Royce Haley. Two more renegades the Rangers can cross off the Fugitive List."

Jim whistled, and an answering whinny rang

out. A moment later Sizzle trotted up to him. The horse nuzzled his face, and dropped his nose to Jim's hip pocket.

"Not you too." Jim chuckled. "One peppermint-beggin' cayuse is enough. Sorry, but I didn't think to bring any candy along. I'll pick some up first town we hit."

"That's some good lookin' bronc," St. Onge said.

"Thanks. You got a shovel in that wagon? Soon as I take care of my horse I'll bury these *hombres*."

"I've got several shovels," St. Onge answered. "In fact, I've got just about anything the hard-working rancher, farmer, or cowhand might need. That's my line, traveling from ranch to ranch selling supplies, sundries, and notions."

"Good. Dig out a couple of those spades while I rub down Sizzle. Long as you don't mind sharin' your campsite, I'll be stopping' here for the night."

"Ranger, after meetin' those two, I'll be plumb grateful for the company," St. Onge replied.

Jim unsaddled and curried his horse, then picketed him on a long line to graze. He shook his head as he hammered the pin into the earth.

"Gotta get used to havin' to tie you when I bed down, Siz. Never had to do that with Sam."

Jim sighed deeply as memories of his days on the trail with Sam flooded back. Sizzle came up behind him and buried his nose in Jim's back, knocking him flat on his face. He nuzzled the back of the prone Ranger's neck.

"All right, let me up, doggone it," Jim yelped, laughing despite himself.

Once Sizzle was settled, Jim and St. Onge buried the two dead outlaws in shallow graves. Rocks were mounded over the graves to discourage scavengers. Jim said a short prayer for the men's souls.

"I was just about ready to cook my supper when those *desperados* rode up on me," St. Onge said as they walked back to the fire. "You ready for some grub?"

"I'm more than ready," Jim answered. "Haven't had any chuck since this morning."

"Then if you'll rustle up some more firewood I'll start the beefsteak and biscuits."

Both men worked quietly, remaining silent while they ate their meal. Once they were finished and lingering over mugs of black coffee, St. Onge finally questioned Jim.

"Lieutenant, you said your name was Blaw . . . ?"

"Bluh-zhick," Jim answered. "It's Polish. Just call me Jim. Most folks do."

"It's easier, that's for certain," St. Onge agreed.

"What about your name? O'Neil St. Onge? That's pretty unusual," Jim said.

"True. Most folks drop the "O" and just call me Neil. My mother was from Ireland, and my father was a Quebecois. So I'm half-Irish and half-French. I'm never certain whether I want to fight or make love." The peddler laughed.

"That can be a problem." Jim chuckled. "Neil, maybe you can help me."

"After you saved my hide? Anything in my stock is yours, Jim."

"Well, I need a new hat," Jim answered, "but that can wait a bit. No, I've got a few questions for you. I'm on the trail of a gang who shot a man and his young boy, then beat and violated his wife and rustled his horses. I've got a lead they might be holed up somewhere along the Pedernales. There would've been six or seven men, and they'd be drivin' a herd of sixteen paint horses and a pair of matched palomino draft horses. Did you happen to meet up with a bunch which might fit that description?"

"I can't say as I have. I do quite a bit of trade all through this territory, but I haven't run across an outfit like that."

Jim dug in his pocket and came up with the scrap of cloth and strands of hair he'd taken from Julia's hand. He showed them to St. Onge.

"You didn't sell anyone a shirt to replace a torn one this color, did you? Or see a man missin' a hunk of sandy hair like this?"

"No, I didn't. Wish I had, and could tell you who bought 'em. But I haven't."

"How about any of the ranches where you've

stopped over the past week or two? You see any paints, especially a blocky tobiano buckskin with a lot of white on his hide?"

"Couple of places along the Pedernales had some paints in their corrals. Nearest one's about fifteen miles upstream from the crossing at Johnson's Settlement. Other one's about five miles beyond that and across the river. Sorry I can't be of more help, Jim. But at least you've got one thing in your favor. Paints aren't all that common around these parts, since most cowpokes don't like those Indian ponies. That should narrow your search some."

"You've been a lot of help, Neil. I'll start at the spreads you just mentioned. Even if neither of 'em are the place I want, maybe they can point me in the right direction."

"I sure hope they can."

"I'll see." Jim shrugged. "I'm gonna get an early start in the morning. Meantime, you said you've got anything a cowpuncher needs in your rig. That include a Stetson in my size?"

"It sure does. C'mon over to the wagon and pick one out. By the way, I also carry several kinds of candy. I believe I heard you tell your horse you'd buy him some peppermints?"

"Here I go again. I can't win." Jim laughed. "All right, dig out some of those."

Jim picked out a new cream-colored Stetson and a light tan shirt. Along with Sizzle's peppermints and some licorice for himself, he took some grain for the horse and two boxes of .45 cartridges.

"How much do I owe you, Neil?" he asked.

"Not a dime, Jim, and don't argue with me!" St. Onge answered, when Jim began to splutter a protest.

"But this stuff cost you considerable," Jim said.

"Not as much as a bullet in my middle would have. Maybe those bullets you just bought will bring down the men who attacked you and your family. That'll be payment enough for me, knowin' in some small way I helped bring them to justice."

"You knew?" Jim exclaimed.

"Not at first. But it wasn't hard to figure," St. Onge explained. "It's in your eyes. Besides, you're riding a paint. I just put two and two together."

"Well, I'll be doggoned! Neil, I'd appreciate it if you didn't let anyone know we'd crossed paths."

"I never saw you, cowboy." St. Onge grinned.

"*Gracias*. Now I'm gonna call it a night. See you at sunup."

"I'll be awake. Always was an early riser," St. Onge said.

Jim checked on Sizzle one last time, giving the paint a peppermint. Sizzle crunched down on the treat, and nuzzled the back of Jim's neck.

He placed his lips to Jim's nose in a horse "kiss."

"You get some rest, pal," Jim said to the gelding. "I've got a hunch we've a long trail ahead. In fact, I'd bet a hat on it."

Jim gave the horse a final pat on the shoulder, then returned to the fire. He spread out his blankets, pulled off his boots and gunbelt, and stretched out. Jim said his evening prayers, and drifted to sleep.

Chapter 11

Two hours after sunup the next day found Jim on the north bank of the Pedernales. The first ranch St. Onge had mentioned was the Box Q, run by an elderly rancher and his wife, their six sons and their wives, and their children. They had indicated they'd seen no sign of the missing horses.

After leaving the Box Q, Jim rested until late afternoon, then waded Sizzle across the shallow rapids of the river. In this section the Pedernales wound between rolling land and grassy flats, which were interspersed by pink granite outcroppings and broken by occasional groves of mesquites, cedars, or oaks. This was ideal grazing country, as well as a location with numerous hiding places for rustled livestock.

Once he'd crossed the river and ridden upstream for six miles, Jim left Sizzle hidden in a mesquite thicket. The Ranger covered the last mile on foot, taking advantage of the dense scrub along the riverbank to reach the second ranch unseen. A soft involuntary whistle escaped from his lips when he saw several of his horses bunched in a corral.

"This is the place, all right," he muttered to

himself. "Not much cover past here, though. And it sure won't be easy to get into that place. That cabin's built like a fort. I'll wait until after dark to hit these *hombres*."

The main building was a sturdy log structure, shaded by several large live oaks. It sat in the middle of a clearing. Off to the left stood a good-sized stable and several corrals.

Jim bellied down to study the terrain. He waited to see if any of the outlaws would show themselves. By the time he backed away from the ranch, he'd determined four or five men were in the well-built cabin.

After spending the rest of the day napping until dusk, then having a cold supper of jerky and hardtack, washed down by river water, Jim rode back to the horse thieves' hideout. He stopped Sizzle just inside the edge of the sheltering brush and tied him loosely to a post oak. He gave the young horse a peppermint, then took a spare bandanna from his saddlebag and tied it around the horse's muzzle. "I'm sorry to do this, Siz, but I can't take any chances on your callin' out and givin' me away," he said. "Wait here until I whistle for you."

Jim left his Winchester in the saddle scabbard, since the rifle would be too awkward to easily maneuver through the dense underbrush. He checked the loads in his Colt, replaced it in his holster, and began working his way through the scrub, aided by the dim light of a waning gibbous moon.

Once he reached the edge of the brush, Jim stopped to again look over the ranch yard before making his final approach. He was about to begin crossing the yard when the cabin door opened and one of the men stepped out. The man headed to one of the trees and stood facing it while he relieved himself.

Jim slid his Bowie knife from its sheath on his belt. He readied the knife for a throw as he stared at the outlaw's broad back, a perfect target in the dim moonlight. He hesitated.

"It'd be real easy to kill that hombre while he's standin' there peein'," Jim thought. "All I gotta do is put my knife in his back."

Jim raised the Bowie, drawing his arm back to fling the heavy-bladed weapon. He stopped with his hand at shoulder height, ready to complete the throw. Despite what the renegades had done to his family, Jim couldn't bring himself to down the man in front of him without warning.

"Texas Ranger!" Jim said. "Don't move. Get your hands up."

The man jumped in surprise, then whirled, hand dropping to the gun on his hip. Jim threw his Bowie, the knife catching the outlaw in his stomach. With a scream the outlaw fell back against the tree, and slid to the dirt.

The cabin door flew open, a man stood in the doorway six-gun drawn. Backlit by the dim light of a lantern inside, he made a clear target.

"Texas Ranger!" Jim shouted. "Throw down that gun!"

The man answered with a bullet which burned along Jim's ribs.

Jim returned fire, his slug taking the silhouetted outlaw in the side. The man jackknifed, exposing another figure behind him. Jim fired again, this time hitting his target in the chest. The man slammed backwards.

Crouched low, Jim raced for the cabin, firing as he went. One of his bullets ripped into the shoulder of a third renegade, spinning him to the floor. Seeing his partners downed, the remaining man threw his gun out the door and raised his hands over his head.

"Don't shoot, Ranger. I quit!"

"Then get over next to your *compadre* and stand hitched."

Jim kept his gun leveled at the man's stomach. He stalked up to the cabin, pausing to check the gut-shot man lying across the sill. The man was unconscious, his breathing ragged. Blood was pooling under his body. He didn't have much time.

Jim checked the second man he'd shot. This renegade was lying on his back, already dead.

The other wounded outlaw was propped against an overturned table, holding his bullet-shattered shoulder.

"Are they dead?" the unhurt horse thief asked.

Jim reloaded his pistol. His blue eyes were colder than ice as he glared at the two surviving men. His voice was low and deadly when he answered.

"They're done for. So's your pardner outside. If you two don't come up with the right answers you'll be joinin' them in the Devil's hop yard plumb quick. What's your name, Mister? And your pard's?"

"It's Prentiss . . . Ben Prentiss." Prentiss nodded toward his wounded partner. "And he's Jules Morton."

"How about the others?"

Prentiss nodded toward the dying man in the doorway.

"That's Hank Peterson. Other's John Holcomb. Mal Bailey's outside."

"Which one of you shot my boy? And which one attacked and raped my wife? Or did all of you do that?"

"What the devil are you talkin' about, Ranger?"

"Don't try and play dumb with me." Jim snarled. "Those are my horses out there in the corral. They were stolen from my ranch a while back. And the outlaws who rustled 'em shot me and my boy, then violated my wife and beat her so badly she may not live. Now tell me which one of you did that or I'll gut-shoot both of you right here and leave you to die real slow. You can bet your hat on it."

"We don't know anything about that," Prentiss said.

Jim swung from the floor catching Prentiss deep in the belly. Prentiss doubled over and Jim punched him square on the nose. Cartilage crunched. The blow flattened Prentiss's nose and brought forth a fountain of blood. Prentiss straightened up and staggered back against the wall. Jim rammed the barrel of his six-gun deep into Prentiss's belly.

"You're lyin'!" Jim growled. He thumbed back the hammer of the heavy Peacemaker.

Prentiss cringed, seeing death in Jim's icy blue eyes.

"I'm not!" he screamed. "We didn't steal those horses. We bought 'em."

"You tellin' me you didn't know those horses were stolen? Don't even think of goin' for that gun! Not one more wiggle!"

Jim shifted the Colt to cover Morton, who had edged toward his dropped revolver. Morton fell back against the table.

"I'm not gonna make another move. But I'm bleedin' to death here, Ranger," he whined.

"You think I care about you *hombres* after what was done to my family?" Jim again rammed the Colt into Prentiss's belly. "You've got ten seconds!"

"I don't know what happened to your wife. Honest. You gotta believe me," Prentiss cried. He was shaking, the sweat pouring down his face mixing with the blood dripping from his broken nose.

"Wrong answer." Jim started to pull the trigger.

"All right, Ranger. Just don't shoot me," Prentiss pleaded. "We knew those horses were stolen, sure. We've been rustlin' livestock for months from around here, and buyin' more from anyone with stuff to sell. We run the stock over to New Mexico or down across the Rio. But we didn't steal those horses or shoot you. And none of us would've shot a boy or attacked a female like you claim. You've got to believe me."

Jim eased back the hammer of his Colt. "All right, say I take your word for it. Unless you want to hang, you'd better be able to tell me who did sell you those horses."

"We got 'em from Reese Macklin and some of his bunch."

"Reese Macklin. I've heard that name. He's wanted for horse and cattle stealin' from the Panhandle clear down to the Rio Grande. He's suspected of several murders too."

"That'd be him. He's a real mean one."

"Where's he hole up when he's not out rustlin'?" Jim demanded.

"Somewhere around Bartlett is what I hear tell," Prentiss answered. "He likes that town because it straddles the county line, so he can keep the sheriffs off his tail just by crossin' the line."

"Rangers don't have that problem," Jim muttered. "County lines don't matter to us. How many in his outfit?"

"There were seven plus Macklin. One of them was real bad shot. Had a bullet in his stomach. Macklin left him here. *Hombre* died the next day. We buried him out back of the barn. Name was Smitty Daniels."

"Another wanted horse thief." Jim grunted.

"Ranger, I gave you what you wanted. You still gonna kill us?" Prentiss asked.

"No. I'll run you both back to Dripping Springs and jail you there."

"If I don't bleed to death first," Morton moaned.

"I'll patch you up in a minute," Jim said. "Prentiss, get on your belly."

"Sure. Whatever you say, Ranger. Just don't plug me."

Prentiss stretched out on the floor.

Jim lifted a piece of rope from a peg and cut it into lengths. He tied Prentiss's hands behind his back, and bound his ankles. "There, that'll hold you," he said. "Now let me take a look at you, Morton."

Jim pulled open the wounded man's shirt. Blood was still seeping from the bullet hole in Morton's shoulder. The Ranger pulled the neckerchief from Morton's neck and wiped away the blood. "I can't dig that bullet out," he said. "It's too deep in the bones. But I can stop the bleedin' until you're back in town and can see a doc."

Jim stepped to the door and whistled. A minute later, Sizzle trotted up to the cabin. He nuzzled Jim's face, and dropped his nose to the Ranger's hip pocket.

Jim pulled the bandanna from Sizzle's nose. He dug out a peppermint and gave it to the horse, then tied him to the rail. He searched his saddlebags for the rudimentary medical kit and small flask of whiskey he carried. Finding what he needed, he went back inside and knelt alongside Morton. He showed no mercy cleaning out the outlaw's wound.

"Ow! Take it a mite easier, will you?" Morton yelped.

"Be grateful I'm even doin' this much for you," Jim snapped back. He poured some of the raw whiskey into the wound. Morton screamed when the fiery liquid bit into the ragged bullet hole.

"Hold still!" Jim ordered. "You're makin' it worse for yourself."

The Ranger stuffed a piece of cloth into the wound, doused it with more whiskey, and bandaged it in place. He tied Morton hand and foot.

"What now?" Prentiss asked.

"I'm gonna check on my horses. Then I'm gonna drag your pardners into the barn so the coyotes can't get to 'em," Jim answered. "After that I'm planning on a good night's sleep. Tomorrow I'll run you into Dripping Springs. And don't get any ideas about tryin' to work loose."

Jim left the cabin. He picked up Sizzle's reins. "All right, boy," he said, "time to rub you down and let you have a reunion with your buddies."

Jim led the paint to the first corral. Sizzle trumpeted a greeting to his corral mates, several of them whinnying in return.

"Ted! Thank you, Lord," Jim exclaimed when he saw Charlie's pet paint gelding push his way through the milling horses and up to the fence. "How you doin', fella? Charlie's sure gonna be glad to see you."

Jim pulled the saddle and bridle from Sizzle and turned the horse into the corral to roll. Then he went through the enclosure, checking on his horses. They were all there, even Ben and Jerry, the wagon horses. In addition, the corral held several more horses which bore the Slash Double E brand. They evidently were also stolen.

Once he'd rubbed down Sizzle, Jim headed to the barn, where he found a half-full grain bin.

He took several buckets of feed to the corral and spread them out for the horses. He forked hay into the enclosure and checked the water troughs. Before leaving he scratched each animal's ears.

The horses cared for, Jim headed back to the cabin. He dragged the bodies of Peterson and Holcomb out of the cabin and into the barn where he loaded them into a buckboard he found there.

At the oak Jim pulled his knife from Mal Bailey's stomach and wiped the blade clean on the dead man's shirt, then stuck it in his belt. He dragged the body into the barn and tossed it in the buckboard alongside the others.

Returning to the cabin he checked Prentiss's and Morton's bonds, and then poured a cup of thick, lukewarm coffee from the pot on the stove. He settled in a chair and glared at the two outlaws.

"I've got your pards loaded in a buckboard," he said. "Tomorrow Prentiss, you're gonna drive that wagon into town while I herd the horses along. Make one false move and there'll be a bullet in your back. Bet a hat on it. And that goes for tonight, too. I'm a real light sleeper, especially when I'm guardin' a couple of wolves."

Jim downed the dregs from his mug and set it aside. He pulled off his shirt, then cleaned and bandaged the shallow bullet crease along his ribs. He stretched out on a bunk in the corner, six-gun in hand, immediately falling into a light slumber.

A half-hour later, when Morton rolled onto his side, Jim was instantly awake. He leveled his Colt at the renegade.

"I just was tryin' to get a bit more comfortable," Morton said.

"Long as that's all you were tryin'," Jim answered. Satisfied Morton and Prentiss would stay put, he drifted back to sleep.

Chapter 12

Sheriff Jesse Gabbard leaned against the fence of Joe Walier's main corral. He'd just returned from a report of stolen horses at the Rafter M ranch and had put his roan gelding back in the pen. "It's a warm one today, Joe, that's for certain," he said to Walier.

"Might be a little rain later to cool things down a bit," Walier answered.

The sheriff jerked upright at the sound of approaching hoof beats accompanied by a thick cloud of dust. "What the devil is that?" he shouted.

"Seems to be some horses comin'," Walier replied.

"Who'd be drivin' in a herd that size?"

"At the rate they're comin', we'll know soon enough," Walier said.

Both men stood gazing to the end of the street.

"Well, I'll be . . . ," Gabbard exclaimed as the horses came into view. "I don't believe what I'm seein'."

"Well I sure do," Walier said grinning. "There's only one man in these parts who can handle horses like that, and that's Jim Blawcyzk."

"But who's that with him, drivin' that buckboard?"

As the herd drew closer, Jim called out to the stable owner. "Open the gate, Joe!"

Walier waved in response and opened the gate to the main corral. Jim pushed the horses inside, and Walier shut the gate behind them.

Jim nodded to Gabbard. "Got a couple of prisoners for you, sheriff. One of 'em needs to see the doc. Got three bodies for the undertaker too."

Gabbard pulled his gun and aimed it at Prentiss. He climbed onto the seat, alongside the outlaw, and glanced at the wounded man lying in the back with the three dead renegades. "Just ease this rig on down to the jail, Mister. I'll get the doc for your friend once you're settled in that cell."

"I'll be along in a while, Jess," Jim said. "You'll have to hold these *hombres* for trial. Rustlin', horse stealin', and receivin' stolen property are the charges so far."

"Not murder?" Gabbard asked.

"Not yet anyway. These aren't the men who attacked my place. They just bought the horses. I'm headin' after the men I really want soon as I finish up here in town."

Gabbard looked over the horses milling in the corral. "Looks like there's some Slash Double E broncs mixed in with your stock," he said.

"You recognize that brand? I'm not familiar with it."

"I'm not either," Gabbard admitted, "But I'll look it up and have the information by the time you reach my office."

"*Bueno*. I won't be long here," Jim said.

"See you shortly." Gabbard stuck his six-gun in Prentiss's ribs. "All right you, let's get movin'. And don't take any bounces. If you do my gun just might go off."

Once the buckboard started toward the jail, Jim climbed out of his saddle. He led Sizzle to the trough and let him drink his fill, then tied him to the rail. The paint nuzzled Jim's neck. He dropped his nose to the Ranger's hip pocket.

"You and your peppermint," Jim said digging in his pocket.

"Let me get you a cup of coffee, Jim?" Walier said. "You sure look as if you could use one."

Jim and Walier went into the horse trader's spacious office. Jim sat in a cane backed chair, tilting it against the wall. Walier took two mugs from a shelf and filled them with coffee from the pot he always kept simmering on the corner stove. He handed one to the Ranger. "I see you got a new hat," he said. "It looks good on you."

"Thanks, Joe, and thanks for your lead. It took me right to those thievin' sidewinders. Now I've gotta ask you to hold the horses here until those two renegades come to trial. They're evidence.

The state'll pay for their board. And since most of those broncs are mine I sure wouldn't trust anyone else to look after 'em."

"You won't have to worry about them," Walier assured the Ranger. "But are you certain about going after those other outlaws? You're looking pretty pale, Jim. I'd wager you've got a fever."

"Don't worry about me!" Jim near spat out the words and then realized how he sounded. "I'm sorry, Joe. I didn't mean to bite your head off. I'm just a mite tired, that's all. I'll grab some chuck and rest a couple of hours before I head out, so I'll be fine."

"I hope you're right, Jim. I'd sure hate to see anything happen to you."

"I appreciate that, Joe. Anything crop up while I was up on the Pedernales that I should know about?"

"Not much. Smoky McCue came by askin' for your whereabouts."

"You didn't tell him where I was headed, did you?"

"I had to," Walier said. "He threatened to haul me in for obstructing justice if I didn't. So I pointed him in the same general direction you went, but without being too specific. I'm sorry, Jim."

"Don't worry about it. You did what you could." Jim scratched the stubble on his face. "So that means ol' Smoke's on my trail."

"Maybe he's still searching for you up along the Pedernales."

"Smoke won't be fooled for long. He'll be on my tail before you know it. Bet a hat on it. I'd best get a move on. Oh, and I'll need one more favor. Could you wait two days, and then send a telegram to Ranger Headquarters tellin' them my horses have been recovered and are here? And make sure to mention Charlie's gelding is with them and doin' fine."

"I can do that, sure, but what about that meal and rest?" Walier asked.

"I can't chance takin' the time with McCue searchin' for me. I'll stop by Jesse's office to take care of the paperwork on those prisoners. After that, I'll grab some grub and supplies at the general store, and ride out."

"Which way are you headed?"

"Joe, I'm not gonna tell you. That way you can honestly say to Smoky when he returns that you have no idea where I was goin'. You won't have to lie, and that'll keep you out of trouble."

"I still wish you'd reconsider." Walier looked worried.

"I can't. I won't rest until the ones who hurt my family are dead."

"Then I guess there's nothing else to say but *Adios*. And be careful, Jim." Joe Walier stuck out his hand.

"Thanks, Joe. For everything."

Jim pulled himself back into the saddle. Less than an hour after taking his leave of Joe Walier, he had his big paint loping northeastward.

It was late in the afternoon when Smoky rode back into Dripping Springs. Not too long after Jim had left town. When Smoky hauled his steeldust gelding up short he spied Jim's stolen horses in Joe Walier's corral. McCue swung out of his saddle and stalked into the barn.

"Joe, Joe Walier!"

"I'm in my office, Smoky. C'mon inside."

"Never you mind that," McCue shouted back. "How long's Jim been back in town? Don't try and deny it. His rustled horses are in your corral."

"I'm not denying a thing," said Walier. "Jim got back early this afternoon with two prisoners and the bodies of three rustlers he'd shot."

"Where's he at now?" Smoky demanded.

"I don't know," Walier responded. "The men he brought in weren't the ones who attacked his ranch. He stayed long enough to turn them over to the sheriff, then he rode out again. He refused to tell me where he was headed."

"You'd better not be lyin' to me, Joe."

"I'm not. Didn't I point you on the right course when I sent you to the Pedernales?"

"You did, although your directions were a mite off," Smoky said. "But once I ran across a bunch of fresh horse tracks I had a gut feelin' they were

125

Jim's horses. I sure didn't expect to find them in your corral, though." He gazed at the horse trader. "You're sure Jim didn't give you any idea where he was headed?"

"Not a hint. He wouldn't tell Jesse Gabbard, either. But how about the prisoners? Jim must've found out from them where the men he's after hole up. You might ask them."

"That's a good idea, Joe. And I'll make 'em talk, one way or another."

"You gonna head right out after that?"

"I sure am. But my horse needs some feed and water. Would you grain him while I'm down at the sheriff's office?"

"I'll do that," Joe said.

Smoky and Walier headed back outside. Smoky lifted Soot's reins from the rail to lead the steeldust inside. He stopped when he saw the Slash Double E horses mixed in with Jim's stock.

"Joe, were those other broncs also rustled?" he asked.

"They were. Nobody seems to know who owns them, though. None of us are familiar with that brand."

"That Slash Double E blaze-faced bay looks familiar. Think I'll take a closer look at him. I want to check those brands anyway."

"I'll take care of your horse while you do." Walier led the gelding into the barn.

Smoky ducked under the rail and up to the bay

gelding. He spoke in soft tones to the horse while he ran a hand down its shoulder, then examined an old scar on its neck.

"I thought so. You're Kurt Stoneham's old bronc. I always did wonder what had happened to you."

Smoky turned away from the horse straight into a vicious punch to his belly which jolted the air from his lungs. He began to fold when a second punch to his jaw straightened him. He staggered back against the fence. Through blurred vision he saw his attacker go for his gun. Before the gunman could clear leather, Smoky lunged forward and sank his fist into the man's gut. With a whoof of expelled air, the man doubled over and went to his knees, gagging. Smoky grabbed his wrist and wrenched the gun from his hand. He pulled his own Colt and leveled it at the man's chest.

His assailant was a youth of no more than sixteen or seventeen. Smoky's blow had knocked the boy's hat from his head, revealing a shock of dark curly hair.

"Don't make a move unless you want a slug clean through you," Smoky ordered. "Why were you tryin' to plug me, boy?"

Arms wrapped around his lean belly, the kid gasped for air. Tears of pain streaked his cheeks. He glared up at the Ranger, his eyes glittering with fury. " 'Cause . . . cause I vowed to kill the men who shot my pa and stole our horses. Since I found you first, I figured to start with you."

"Wait a minute, son. You've made a mistake. I'm no horse thief. I'm a Texas Ranger. I'm on the trail of my pardner, who's after the same bunch."

"Then what're you doin' with our horses?"

"You're a stubborn cuss, ain't ya, kid?" Smoky half-smiled. "I'm a Ranger. I was checkin' their brands. Those Slash Double E broncs yours?"

"Yeah, they are."

"What's your name, son?"

"Eric Esposito."

Smoky pulled the boy to his feet. Eric was tall, almost as tall as Jim Blawcyzk, and extremely lanky. It was hard for the Ranger to believe a kid that thin could have hit him so hard his guts still ached.

"Well, Eric, you've got plenty of sand, I'll give you that," Smoky said. He rubbed his sore belly. "And for a skinny kid you pack a mean wallop. But you might want to make sure who you're dealin' with before you just go chargin' in next time. You'll live a lot longer that way."

"I reckon you're right. Sorry, Ranger."

"Call me Smoky. You say the men who stole your horses shot your pa?"

"Yeah, they did. They bushwhacked him. Drilled him in the back. Lucky for my pa the bullet took him high, plus it missed his spine.

He's gonna be laid up a while, but the doc says he'll be all right."

"Where's your spread at?"

"It's a day's ride or so outside of Bartlett. That's about seventy miles northeast of here."

Joe Walier appeared in the barn doorway. "Everything all right out here, Smoky?" he asked.

"Yep, it sure is," Smoky replied. "This here's Eric Esposito of the Slash Double E. He was trailin' his horses. Eric, this is Joe Walier. He owns this stable."

"Pleased to meet you, sir."

"Not sir, Joe. And I'll say the same."

"Joe, I'd imagine Eric'll want to take his horses back home. How much'll he owe you?"

"He won't owe me a dime, but I'm afraid he can't have his horses quite yet. They're being held as evidence until those two men Jim arrested come to trial. The circuit judge isn't due for at least three weeks, so the horses have to stay here until then. Meantime, the state is paying for their board."

"You mean two of the men who shot my pa are in jail here?"

"No, the men Jim brought in bought the horses from the *hombres* who did the rustling. Jim is still after the real thieves."

"Joe, I've got an idea Eric might be able to help me find those men. I'm gonna head down to the sheriff's office now, and take him along. Eric, where's your horse?"

"He's hidden right around the corner, in the alley alongside the millinery shop."

"Get him. Joe, take care of the kid's horse, will you? Once we're done with Jesse, we'll be riding out."

"Sure thing," said Walier.

"C'mon, kid," Smoky said. "I think we'll know right soon where to look for those rustlers."

Chapter 13

Jim found a good campsite and stopped about two hours before sunset. There was plenty of grass for his horse and a small pond for water. He cared for Sizzle and took a swim, then made his supper. Relaxing alongside his campfire with a cup of coffee he was gazing at Sizzle when the paint looked up and snuffed softly. He stood stock still, his ears pricked forward.

"Someone comin', Siz? Or is it just a coyote or javelina slinkin' through the brush?" Jim stood up and scanned the horizon in the direction of the horse's gaze.

A moment later, Sizzle nickered a soft welcome.

"Well, whoever it is you're not worried about him. Of course, you're never worried about anything." Jim chuckled.

"Jim, is that you?" A familiar voice called out.

"Smoky. I should've known," Jim muttered in disgust. "Yeah, Smoke, it's me. Ride on in."

Smoky and Eric appeared from behind the thin screen of brush sheltering Jim's campsite. As usual, a cigarette was dangling from Smoky's lips. They reined in their horses and stepped down from their saddles.

131

"Boy howdy, you led me a chase for fair, Jim," Smoky said trying to hide a grin.

"Yeah, but you found me."

"I reckon that's so," Smoky agreed.

"Who's the kid?"

"This here's Eric Esposito. His folks own the Slash Double E outside of Bartlett. Those were their horses you brought in along with your own. Eric, this ugly galoot is Lieutenant Jim Blawcyzk of the Texas Rangers. We've been ridin' pards for years."

"Pleased to meet you, Lieutenant."

Jim took the boy's hand in a firm grip. "Same here, Eric." He turned back to McCue. "How'd you find me so quick? I didn't tell anyone in Dripping Springs where I was headed, not even the sheriff. Don't tell me Jim Huggins is with you and helped track me down. Cap'n Trumbull said he was puttin' him on this case."

"Huggins isn't with me. He got wounded by a rustler outside San Angelo. Shot in the side. Jim killed the *hombre* that plugged him. Huggins'll be fine, but he had to go home for some rest."

"So how'd you locate me? No one had any idea where I was headed."

"Those men you brought in knew. It wasn't hard to persuade them to tell me which way you went."

"I should've figured."

"Jim, I reckon you know why I'm here."

"I reckon I do, but why don't you tell me?"

"Cap'n Trumbull wants me to bring you back to Austin. He's mighty angry. Claims you disobeyed orders."

Jim shook his head. "Smoke, why don't you just ride on back to Austin and tell the captain you couldn't find me?"

"You know I can't do that, Jim. Besides, I've got a message for you. Charlie took a turn for the worse after you left. He's got an infection, and maybe blood poisoning."

"Smoke, we've been saddle pards a long time. I know you wouldn't lie to me about my boy. But the last thing Charlie said to me was that he wanted me to find the men who hurt him and his mother, no matter what. What happens to Charlie and Julia is in the Lord's hands. I'm sure hoping He'll let them recover, but that's His will, and nothing I do can change that. But I can hunt down the renegades who attacked my family and make sure they don't hurt anyone else. I won't be turning back until that's done."

"Jim, I can't let you do that."

Smoky laid a hand on Jim's shoulder. Jim whirled and drove a straight right into Smoky's jaw. Smoky staggered backwards. Jim closed in, but Smoky ducked his next punch and sank his right into Jim's belly. He followed that with a left to Jim's chin, then a right to the ribs. Jim dropped to one knee, gasping for breath.

Smoky headed in, intending to knock Jim out with a final blow to the back of his neck. Instead Jim parried the blow and shot a punch to Smoky's liver. Half-paralyzed by the blinding pain Smoky spun around and crumpled.

"Had enough, Smoke?" Jim said.

"Not quite," Smoky rasped. "I'm still gonna take you in, pard."

Jim kicked him in the belly. Smoky collapsed to his face, shuddered once, and lay still.

Jim picked up his Stetson from where it had fallen, stumbled over to the pond, and filled the hat. Weaving with every step, he staggered back to his downed partner and poured the contents of the hat over Smoky's face. Smoky spluttered, shocked back to his senses by the cold liquid.

Jim sat down next to his partner. "You still gonna try'n take me back to Austin, corporal?"

"I reckon not. It'd probably be a better idea to go along and give you a hand, before you get yourself killed by those renegades you're after."

"You'll get in Dutch with Cap'n Trumbull."

"I'll worry about him after we round up those outlaws."

"Now you're sounding more like my pard, Smoke." Jim's attempt at a grin came out as more of a grimace.

Smoky moaned and sat up. He rubbed his

swollen jaw, and ran a hand over his battered face.

"That's if either of us is in any shape to ride."

"We've ridden in worse shape," Jim said.

"I guess you're right. And it's too bad the rest of the boys couldn't have seen that fight. They've always wanted to see what'd happen if me and you ever got into it."

"Dunno about you, but I don't aim to let that happen again," Jim said. "This one just about finished me."

"Same here," Smoky agreed. "I guess we'd better try and patch ourselves up, best we can."

"I thought you Rangers were supposed to try and find the men who shot my pa and rustled our horses, not kill each other," said Eric frowning. "There's still three hard days ridin' to Bartlett, but at this rate you'll both be dead before we make another twenty miles."

"The kid's right, Smoke," Jim said. "Pardners again?"

"Pardners again."

"Eric," said Jim, "why don't you start a fire and begin supper while Jim and I clean up? There's food in my saddlebags. Cookin' utensils too."

"Sure thing," Eric answered.

Jim forced himself to his feet and walked to his saddle. He rummaged in his saddlebags until he came up with a bar of harsh yellow soap, a tin of witch hazel, another of salve, and a small towel.

While Eric searched for more firewood, Jim and Smoky headed for the pond.

"I reckon there's not much use of holdin' onto what's left of these shirts," Smoky said grinning. Both his and Jim's had been ripped to shreds in their fight.

"I reckon not." Jim laughed.

They peeled off the remnants of the garments and tossed them aside. Then they stretched out on their bellies to duck their battered faces in the cooling water.

The partners washed up thoroughly, scrubbing themselves with the soap, despite its sting on their raw cuts, then rinsing out their wounds with the witch hazel and coating them with salve. Once they had dried off, they retrieved spare shirts from their saddlebags and shrugged into them.

Eric cooked up a mess of bacon and beans, which the trio eagerly devoured, Jim downing more grub despite having previously eaten. Once the meal was finished, they relaxed around the dying fire. Smoky rolled and lit a cigarette.

"Jim, Eric told me the men who stole his horses and wounded his pa were most likely the Macklin bunch. His family's ranch is a day's ride outside of Bartlett. Reese Macklin holes up around there somewhere. Same outfit you're after, if those prisoners back in Jesse Gabbard's cell told me the truth."

"That's who I'm after, all right," Jim said. "Eric, you have any idea where Macklin's hideout might be?"

"Not a clue. Those boys hit real fast, then disappear. No one's ever been able to trail 'em."

"That's about to change. You said we have three days hard ridin' ahead of us before we reach Bartlett?"

"That's about right," Eric said.

"We're gonna make it in two. You figure your horse can keep up?"

"Ol' Blue'll do just fine."

"Good. We'll be ridin' out before sunup. Time to get us some shut-eye."

Eric doused the fire. The men rolled in their blankets. Worn out, they were soon asleep, so exhausted even the pain of their bruises couldn't keep Smoky and Jim from slumber. Jim fell asleep before the recitation of his evening prayers was half complete.

Chapter 14

Late in the afternoon two days later, the trio rode into the small town of Bartlett. No one paid any attention to the trail-stained, dust covered riders and their mounts. Unlike most Texas Rangers, who didn't wear badges, Jim and Smoky carried silver star on silver circle emblems they'd hand carved from Mexican ten peso coins. However, they usually kept them out of sight, hidden in their pockets until needed. Jim hadn't shaved, had a haircut, or bathed since he'd left San Leanna, so his blonde hair hung over his collar and blonde whiskers stubbled his jaw. Smoky and Eric didn't look all that much better. Smoky's silver-tipped black hair appeared even frostier than usual under its coating of dust. There was nothing to distinguish them from any other drifting cowpunchers. A few people did stare at the splendid paint gelding between Jim's legs. Even after all the hard miles, Sizzle's hide still gleamed like a newly-minted penny under its layer of dust, and he still stepped along smartly, showing no sign of weariness.

Jim and Smoky's eyes were in constant motion under their pulled-down Stetsons. Their gazes missing little that went on around them.

"There's the sheriff's office just ahead," Jim said. "Reckon we'd better check in with him before we settle our broncs for the night."

"You sure, Jim?" Smoky asked. "We usually don't do that right off."

"I know but Eric's known in this town. 'Sides, it doesn't really matter. I'd just as soon those renegades know I'm comin' after 'em."

They reined up in front of the ramshackle building holding the office and jail. When they did, a youngster of about six leveled a toy wooden six-gun at them from his perch on the hitchrail. He had a paper sheriff's badge pinned to his shirtfront.

"Hands up, outlaws, or I'll shoot you right in your bellies," he ordered.

"Reckon he's got the drop on us, men." Jim chuckled. "Better listen to him before he drills us."

He raised his hands shoulder high. Smoky and Eric followed suit.

"All right, you've got us. We'll go peaceable-like," Jim said. "What's your name, Sheriff?"

"It's Tommy. Tommy Pascale Kergaravat," the boy answered.

"That's quite a mouthful," Smoky said. "A man could get shot before he spit that whole handle out."

"You keep quiet, Mister. Now step off those horses."

Sizzle stretched out his neck, nuzzled the boy's chest, then licked his face. Unprepared for the gelding's huge pink tongue swiping across his face, Tommy tumbled backward onto the boardwalk.

Jim swung out of his saddle and hurried to the fallen youngster. He pulled the boy to his feet. "Are you all right, son?"

"Sure. I'm fine." Tommy sniffled. "Why'd your horse do that?"

"He was just sayin' hello. Sometimes Sizzle's too friendly for his own good."

Sizzle again nuzzled Tommy's chest.

"See, now he's sayin' he's sorry."

Tommy patted the horse's velvety muzzle.

"You still gonna arrest us, Sheriff?" Smoky asked from atop Soot.

"I reckon not," Tommy replied. "But how about I watch your cayuses for you? There's plenty of horse thieves in these parts."

"Sure," Jim agreed. "How much to keep your eye on 'em?"

"Four bits?"

"The horse thieves ain't the only crooks around here," Smoky said grumbling in jest.

"That's for all three broncs, right Tommy?" Jim asked.

"Yessir."

"Then that's fine." Jim dug in his pocket, came up with two quarters, and handed them to the

140

boy. "Make sure no one comes near them now," he warned.

"You can count on me!" Tommy answered.

Smoky and Eric dismounted. All three men tied their horses, then stepped inside the sheriff's office.

A middle-aged man wearing a sheriff's star on his cowhide vest looked up from behind his newspaper as they entered the office. "Help you gents?" he began, then came to his feet when he recognized the boy. "Eric! You made it back. Your ma'll sure be glad to see you. Your pa's doin' right well. Did you get your horses back? And who're these fellers you're with?"

"Easy sheriff, one question at a time," Eric said. "Thanks for lettin' me know about Pa. I'll be back home at the ranch tomorrow night. Far as these men, they're Texas Rangers. The tall one found my horses. They're in Dripping Springs right now, in state custody. Now these Rangers are after the men who shot Pa and stole 'em."

The sheriff eyed Smoky and Jim. "Rangers, huh?"

"That's right," Jim answered. "I'm Lieutenant Jim Blawcyzk, and this is my pardner, Corporal Smoky McCue."

"I'm sure glad to see some Rangers in town," the lawman answered. "I'm Lee Pierce." He shook both men's hands with a firm grip.

Pierce was tall and stocky, his somewhat thick jowls framed by a silver beard and mustache.

"You said your name was Blah . . . ?"

"Bluh-zhick," Jim explained. "It's Polish. Easier to just call me Jim."

"And I'm Smoky," McCue added, looking up from the quirly he was rolling.

"Then I'm Lee," the sheriff responded. "I take it you boys are on the trail of Reese Macklin and his bunch."

"You're right," Jim said. "We're gonna rest up here for the night, get Eric back home, then light out on their trail. You wouldn't have any idea where we can find them, would you?"

"That's an easy question," Pierce replied. "Those boys don't bother to hide their tracks on their own stompin' grounds. There's a little town called Buckholts about eighteen miles northeast of here. Macklin's place is just beyond that. He pretty much runs things in Buckholts. And before you ask, he's never done a thing against the law in Bell, Williamson, or Milam counties. So none of us county sheriffs have any reason to go after him."

"County lines mean nothing to the Texas Rangers," Smoky said. "We'll get those renegades, sheriff."

"Well, I don't envy you havin' to take on that bunch," Pierce replied.

"Meantime," said Jim, "that growlin' you hear

142

ain't a bear. It's my belly remindin' me it's been far too long since I had a good meal. Where's the best place for grub in this town?"

"A young fella just opened up a new place coupla' months back, called Jersey Marc's. That's Marc with a c when you're lookin' for the sign. It's two blocks south of here. He serves up the best chuck this side of Texarkana."

"Lee, how about a place to cut some of the dust from our gullets?" Smoky asked.

"That'd be the Frog Rock Saloon, a block past Marc's place. You can't miss it. It's got a big boulder shaped like a frog out front. Bill Handy, who owns the place, even painted that rock green and with frog's eyes."

Pierce glanced at the calendar on the opposite wall. "You boys are in real luck," he added. "Therese Marchitto's entertainin' at the Frog Rock tonight. You won't want to miss her show. Sure wish I could be there, but my wife Cathy'll skin me alive if I don't get home on time for once."

"We'll be turnin' in early, Lee," Jim said.

"You do look a mite tired, Jim. But I'd recommend you stay for at least the first show," Pierce said. "I guarantee if you do you'll have sweet dreams all night long."

"Maybe we'll take your advice then," Jim answered.

"We're going to," Smoky added.

143

"Glad to hear that," Pierce responded. "How about a room for the night?"

"We're gonna see if we can bunk in the loft at the livery stable. That's always cheaper than a hotel, plus a lot of times it's cleaner. And it's convenient to have our horses handy."

"I can't argue with you there," Pierce said. "Anything else I can do for you?"

"Maybe you can," Jim answered. "Be right back." He headed outside where Tommy was still standing guard over the horses. "I see you're still on the job," Jim said.

"That's right, Mister," Tommy answered.

Jim retrieved the piece of fabric, strands of hair, and ruined Stetson and shirt from his saddlebags. He returned to the office and passed them to Pierce for his scrutiny. "You recognize any of these, Lee?"

"I'm not sure. That Stetson resembles one Clete King wears. The shirt's about his size too. He's been rumored to ride with the Macklin gang. Used to have a small horse ranch just outside of town here, but the bank took it and he hasn't been seen since. And that sandy-colored hair is a match for Macklin's."

"That just might be a big help. Thanks, sheriff. Now I reckon we'll settle our broncs and get supper."

"Since you'll be headin' out early, if I don't see you, good luck."

"Appreciate that," Jim said. "And thanks for your help."

"Anytime."

The Rangers and Eric stepped outside to find Tommy stroking Sizzle's nose.

"I see you didn't let any horse thieves get our mounts." Jim grinned.

"That's right. I sure didn't. But here comes one now."

Tommy stiffened and yanked the toy pistol from his belt. He leveled it at an approaching figure.

"You're not stealin' any horses I'm watchin', Rog," he shouted. "Bang! Gotcha, ya lowdown varmint. Plugged ya dead center."

Tommy's target, an older boy who bore a strong resemblance to him, clutched his chest, screeched, and pitched to his face.

"Told ya I'd keep your horses safe," Tommy said to the Rangers. "I shot that no-good horse thief for you. He's done for."

"Thomas, what are you doing?" a pleasant featured woman called. Alongside her was a ruggedly handsome man, next to him a pretty young girl. "And Roger, get up out of that road," she ordered.

"All right, Mom." The "dead" young horse thief pushed himself to his feet.

The woman hurried up to where the Rangers and Eric stood smiling. "I hope my boy hasn't been troubling you gentlemen," she said.

"Not at all, ma'am," Jim replied, grinning. "Tommy's been watching our horses for us. And he's done a fine job. Just killed himself a horse thief."

"I'm no horse thief," Roger protested.

"Yes, you are!" Tommy dug out his toy gun and shoved the barrel into Roger's belly. "Blam! Nailed ya right in your guts. You're dead for sure this time."

Roger grabbed his middle and crumpled to the sidewalk.

"Ya killed me all right," he groaned.

"Hey! That's enough foolishness out of the both of you," their mother said frowning.

"And I'll bet he charged you for watching your mounts," the man said when he reached the group. "My son's always trying that whenever we're in town. I'm Roger Kergaravat . . . Senior. That supposed horse thief Tommy just shot dead is his older brother, Roger Junior. And these fine ladies are my wife Wendy and daughter Paige."

"We're pleased to meet all of you," Jim replied introducing himself and his riding companions.

"Please forgive my brothers for their crude behavior," Paige sniffed. "They certainly don't know how to act in town."

"They're just practicin' to be Texas Rangers when they grow up," Smoky said.

"Roger Kergaravat. Seems to me I met a feller

by that name down in Sanderson a few years back," said Jim.

"That'd be me," Roger spoke up. "I remember you now, Lieutenant."

"Roger's right. We moved here from Sanderson about two years ago," Wendy added.

"We have a small ranch about two miles east of town," Roger, Senior said. "I run a few head of cattle and grow garden truck. We've done quite well."

"I'm glad to hear that," Jim responded.

"Are you going to be in this area long?" Wendy asked. "If you are, we'd be pleased to have you stop by for supper."

"Only for tonight, I'm afraid," Jim answered. "We're after the Macklin bunch. We'll be riding out first thing."

"It's about time someone went after them," Wendy said, her teeth clenched. "A woman isn't safe with them around. Reese Macklin accosted me once. Luckily Roger came home before anything happened and chased him off. I won't even let Paige ride her pony alone until something is done about them."

A deep sadness crossed Jim's countenance. "I have to say that's only too accurate, Mrs. Kergaravat," he replied. "No one is safe with Reese Macklin and his men on the loose. But those *hombres* won't be a menace much longer. I promise you that."

"I told my mom I can take care of myself," Paige insisted.

"I'm sure you can, but your mom is right. Those men are too dangerous," Jim told her.

"Well, we certainly wish you Rangers luck," the elder Kergaravat said. "And my wife's invitation stands. You'd be welcome at our place anytime. It's the Circle K. Located on the Davilla road just east of Bartlett. You can't miss it."

"If we get the chance to stop by we certainly will," Jim answered. "After all, we know our horses are safe with Tommy guardin' them."

"Not any longer, he won't be," Roger shouted. He pulled out his own toy gun and aimed it at his brother's back. "Bang!"

Tommy yelped, then slumped to the dirt.

"Now I can steal all the horses I want with the sheriff dead," Roger said. "Rob them banks too!"

"I wouldn't try that with two Texas Rangers right here," Paige warned.

"I reckon you're right, Sis. I was just kiddin'."

"We'd better get going if we're to make it home before dark, honey," Wendy told her husband.

"You're right," he agreed. "Rangers, hope to see you again. *Adios*."

Chapter 15

Once their horses were cared for and arrangements to spend the night in the livery stable loft completed, Jim, Smoky, and Eric washed up in the trough behind the stable, then headed for Jersey Marc's.

"Boy howdy, I never thought I'd see the day when a livery stable hostler could handle your horse for you, Jim," Smoky remarked while they strolled toward the restaurant. "I can hardly wait to get back to some of the stables Sam's torn up in the past and see the looks on the owners' faces when you walk in leadin' Sizzle. I'll bet most of 'em faint dead away."

"Who's Sam?" Eric asked.

"The meanest, toughest bronc who ever lived in the state of Texas," Smoky answered.

"And he's also the finest cayuse a Ranger ever rode, and my best friend," Jim said. "He saved my life a heap of times. But one of the same bunch who shot your dad and stole your horses tried to take Sam. Sam's a one-man horse, and wouldn't stand for it. Looks like he half-killed the *hombre*, but he was hurt real bad fightin' him off. He'll be crippled the rest of his life."

"I'm sure sorry, Jim," Eric answered.

"Thanks, son. Well, here's the restaurant."

The threesome climbed the stairs to Jersey Marc's. As soon as they stepped inside the café the owner called out a hearty greeting.

"Welcome, gentlemen. I'm Jersey Marc, the proprietor of this fine establishment. Find yourselves a seat and I'll be right with you."

Jim chose a red-checked, cloth covered corner table where he and his companions had a good view of the front door and no windows at their backs.

"He's a right cheery cuss," Smoky muttered, settling into his chair. "Man, it sure smells good in here."

The small restaurant was redolent with the delectable smells of frying meat and potatoes.

Marc hurried over. He was a stocky individual, slightly moon-faced, with dark, close cropped hair and dark eyes that sparkled with energy.

"What'll you have, gents?" he inquired. "I've got my own specialty which is quite good, if you'll allow me to boast. It's beefsteak sliced really thin, then fried to a turn. That's accompanied with potatoes, sliced thin and fried to a crisp. There's also fresh green beans today and homemade bread, of course. If you'd like dessert later I've made a fresh batch of sugar cookies."

"Sounds good to me," Jim said. "How about you boys?"

"Same here," Smoky replied.

"Me too," Eric agreed.

"Three double orders," said Jim, "and a pot of black coffee."

"I'll have them for you in a jiffy," Marc promised. He hurried off to begin preparing their supper. A moment later he returned with a pot of coffee and three mugs.

"That's a pretty unusual handle you've got there—Jersey Marc," Jim noted.

Marc shrugged. "I'm from New Jersey. I worked for a man named Mike up there who owned a couple of restaurants in a shoreline town. He called the places 'Jersey Mike's.' When I decided to come to Texas and strike out on my own I decided to use the name, only substitute my own. I tried to remain just plain Marc, but the Jersey in the restaurant's name stuck to me also. I can't really complain about that. It's sorta free advertising."

"Interesting story," Jim said. "My handle's Jim Blawcyzk, and this is my ridin' pard Smoky McCue. We're Texas Rangers. The boy's Eric Esposito. He's ridin' back home and kinda taggin' along with us."

"I'm pleased to meet all of you," Marc said. "Say, I'd best check on your supper. Wouldn't do to let it burn."

Soon the Rangers and Eric were digging into heaping plates of beef and potatoes. They ate silently, enjoying the change from beans and bacon. When they were finished, Marc brought over a plate piled high with warm sugar cookies. The treats disappeared as if by magic.

"How was everything?" Marc asked.

"It was delicious," Smoky said patting his full stomach. He tilted back in his chair and began puffing on a cigarette.

"More coffee or cookies?"

"No thanks, Marc," Jim answered. "I'd bust if I ate another thing."

"And my poor horse Ol' Blue'd collapse under me if I climbed into the saddle right now," Eric added.

"Besides, we've got to get an early start in the morning," Jim said.

"Not until we head over to the Frog Rock and see that Therese lady Lee Pierce told us about," Smoky reminded him.

"Ah, yes, Therese Marchitto." Marc heaved a sigh. "The woman every man within a hundred miles of here wants, but can't have."

"That good lookin', huh Marc?" Smoky grinned in anticipation.

"You'll see when you get there," Marc answered.

"Then I guess you'd better give us our check."

"Sure thing." Marc hurriedly calculated the bill. The Rangers paid it, downed final gulps of coffee, and pushed back their chairs.

"That was the best meal I've had in a month of Sundays," Smoky declared.

"Yep. Haven't had one that good since leavin' home," Jim agreed. "G'night, Marc."

"Good night, men. And say hello to Therese for me if she'll let you get close enough," Marc answered, a faraway look in his eyes.

Eric tagged along when Jim and Smoky headed for the Frog Rock Saloon.

"This has gotta be the place," Smoky remarked, gazing at the waist high frog shaped rock in front of the establishment. They climbed the stairs to the entrance. At the batwings, Smoky turned and stopped the youngster.

"Whoa, kid, ain't you a mite young to be goin' into saloons?" he demanded.

"I'm sixteen," Eric protested. "That's old enough to join the Texas Rangers, and old enough to drink in a saloon if I want to. I've been in this place before. Besides, you ain't my pa. You can't stop me."

"Jim, don't you have anythin' to say here?"

"Not a thing I can say, Smoke. Eric's right. He can go in saloons if he wants to, and we sure aren't his ma or pa. It's his privilege to do what he wants."

Smoky shrugged. "Okay, but if he gets in trouble he'd better not expect us to bail him out of it."

"Don't bother yourself about that. I'm not lookin' for trouble," Eric said grinning.

The Frog Rock looked like many a Texas

saloon, with two exceptions. It had the usual bar stretching half the length of the back wall, backed by a mirror and shelves full of liquor bottles. A derby-hatted player was torturing the keys of an out of tune piano. Several couples were on a small dance floor, attempting to swirl to the notes. A number of large, gilt-framed pictures of scantily clad women in suggestive poses hung on the walls. And of course there were the ever-present gaming tables, faro setups, a roulette wheel, and chuck-a-luck cages. Percentage girls circulated among the patrons. Tobacco smoke swirled to the ceiling, dimming the light from the coal oil lamps. But what caught the rangers' eyes was the white line painted down the middle of the floor, up to the bar. And that bar had wheels on it.

"What the devil is that all about, Jim?" Smoky said.

"Only one way to find out," Jim replied. He elbowed his way to the bar, clearing a spot for himself and his companions.

"What's your pleasure, gents?" the burly bartender boomed from his place behind the mahogany. "I'm Bill Handy, owner of the Frog Rock. Howdy."

"Howdy," Jim answered. "Just sarsaparilla for me."

"Not a drinkin' man, eh? I can respect that, even though it ain't good for my business." Handy smiled when he said it.

"Rye for me," Smoky said.

"Beer," Eric added.

"Comin' right up." Handy placed a bottle of whiskey and a glass in front of Smoky, drew a mug of beer and placed it in front of Eric, then rummaged under the bar until he came up with two bottles of sarsaparilla. He opened one and handed it to Jim. "Anything else you need?"

"We are a trifle curious about that line down the middle of the floor," said Jim. "And the wheels on your bar."

Handy laughed. "Most strangers who come in here ask about it. That line's the county line. Left side of that's Williamson County. Right side is Bell. Laws are different in each. So whenever a snoopin' lawman takes a notion to come in here lookin' to arrest someone or shut me down for violatin' some stupid rule, we just roll the bar and move the customers to whatever county that lawman ain't from. Since we're out of his jurisdiction, he can't touch us."

"Yeah, but he could sure shoot you," Smoky muttered. "A lead slug doesn't respect county lines."

"Reckon you're right, but that ain't happened yet, stranger."

"And the Texas Rangers don't have to worry about county boundaries. What would occur if a Ranger happened to wander in here?" Jim asked.

"That ain't happened yet," Hardy said grinning.

155

"It has now. You're palaverin' with two Rangers right here."

"You two *hombres* are Rangers? I don't believe it," Hardy retorted.

Jim's blue eyes glittered like chips of ice.

"Rangers Jim Blawcyzk and Smoky McCue at your service."

Handy's Adam's apple bobbed up and down. He spluttered, trying to form a response.

"You . . . you ain't here to close my place down, are you, Ranger?"

"Don't worry," Jim replied. "We're after bigger fish than you, Handy. The Macklin gang. They ever stop in here?"

"Yeah. Yeah, they do on occasion. Ain't been by for a while, though."

"Well, if they should happen to show up tonight you'll point 'em out for us, won't you?"

"I certainly will," Handy stammered.

"Good. Meantime we'll enjoy our drinks. And it looks to me like there's an empty chair or two at your poker tables. Maybe we'll set in on a game while we're waitin' for the show. I understand your female entertainer is really somethin'."

"She surely is," Handy answered. "Her first show's in an hour. Look, why don't I make your next round of drinks on the house? And follow me to the tables. I'll introduce you to my chief houseman. He'll make sure you enjoy yourselves in an honest game."

"We'd appreciate that," Jim said.

Handy led the threesome to a felt-covered table where a man was dealing cards to two ranchers.

"Joe, these men would like to get in on a game. You're looking at Rangers Blawcyzk and McCue." He hesitated when he came to Eric. "Sorry, son, but I never did catch your name."

"Eric Esposito."

"Good. My chief houseman, Joe Piccirillo. He'll see to your needs."

Piccirillo rose from his chair. He was tall and thin, handsome in a swarthy way, his somewhat bony face emphasized by the spade beard he affected. His dark eyes were almost as black as his close-cropped hair. The gambler's hands and fingers were long and slender, perfectly suited to his chosen trade. He wore a black suit, white shirt, black string tie, but was hatless. A diamond ring sparkled on his left pinky.

"Pleased to make your acquaintance, gentlemen," he stated, his voice like silk. "You may join me and these others in our game, if you'd like."

"That suits me fine," said Jim. "Smoke, Eric, what about you?"

"I'm in," Eric said.

"I think I'll buck the faro setup for a while," Smoky replied.

"Certainly. Tell Maxwell over there he's to extend every courtesy."

"I'll tell him." Smoky hesitated. He looked at Jim. "You all right, pardner?" he said. "You're lookin' a mite peaked."

"I'm fine," Jim assured him. "You have some fun. This might be your last chance for a while."

"Thanks." Smoky wandered to the opposite side of the room.

"Gentlemen," said Piccirillo, "these other two players are Hank McCarthy and Don Strothers."

The two ranchers nodded to Jim and Eric as they took their seats.

They had been playing for nearly an hour when Jim pushed back his chair. While he usually enjoyed a good poker game, and had hoped tonight's would help him unwind, he found himself unable to concentrate on the cards. Several times he made obvious blunders that cost him a hand. Now down a few dollars, he decided to call it a night, at least as far as gambling was concerned.

"I'm sorry, gents, but luck's not runnin' my way tonight," he said. "Reckon I'll just have another pop, watch the show, then call it an evening."

"You look pretty tired," said Strothers. "I guess you've been on the trail for some time, eh?"

"And I've got a ways to go yet," Jim answered.

"Therese Marchitto will get your blood stirrin' again," McCarthy said grinning. He glanced at the clock over the piano. "She'll be comin' on

158

any minute now. Looks like your pard's headin' over too."

Smoky flashed a huge roll of yellowbacks.

"Seems like you did all right, Smoke," Jim said.

"All right? I 'bout near busted the bank. How about you?"

"My luck's cold tonight. But Eric's doin' okay for himself."

The youngster had won several pots.

"Well, good for him."

"Quiet! The show's about to start!" Piccirillo whispered.

Bill Handy stepped onto a small stage at the far end of the room. He raised his hands for silence. "Gentlemen, the moment you've all been waiting for. The Frog Rock Saloon is proud to present the Delight of Denton, the Toast of Tyler, the Belle of Bartlett, Therese Marchitto!"

The curtains behind the stage parted. A wave of applause washed over the saloon as a dark-eyed woman stepped onto the stage.

Every man's heart began pounding when Therese Marchitto appeared. She was stunningly beautiful. Her dark eyes and long black hair, which was held in place by a mother of pearl comb with a white lace mantilla, hinted at her Spanish or Mediterranean heritage. Her ruby red lips parted slightly to reveal perfect white teeth. Her gown was blood-red silk, complementing her smooth olive skin and dark features. It was cut low to emphasize her magnificent bosom and spectacular cleavage in which a huge diamond necklace nestled. The dress hugged her gorgeous figure so tightly she seemed to have been poured into it. A slit up one side revealed a long and shapely leg. A matching silk scarf was draped over her shoulders. She stopped, standing motionless, with her arms arched over her head, her gaze tilted toward the floor, the very personification of every man's desire.

Smoky nudged Jim in his ribs. "Look at the kid," he whispered.

"Why?" Even the happily married Blawcyzk didn't want to tear his gaze away from this woman.

"Just look."

Jim took a quick glance at Eric and grinned. The boy's eyes were so wide they appeared ready to pop out of his head.

A Mexican guitar player took his place on stage behind the woman. He paused for a moment, then strummed his first chord, wild, intense, and demanding.

Therese Marchitto commenced a flamenco, slowly and softly clacking the castanets in her hands at first, their speed, rhythm, and intensity increasing along with the dance while she stepped from the stage to work her way around the room.

The temperature inside the Frog Rock seemed

to rise to almost unbearable levels as Therese swirled and gyrated, those castanets in her hands sounding like Gatling gun fire, the tapping of her heels matching their staccato rhythm. The perspiration on her face added a glow, increasing her appeal. She was sultry, inviting, intoxicating, fascination itself. Therese spun, dipped, and whirled in effortless motion. She was passion, power, brute force, all personified in that wild dance. When she tossed her head, that black hair seemed to flow like a silken waterfall. The diamond on her bosom scintillated in the glow of the lights.

Therese moved from table to table, here running her scarf over a man's shoulders, there placing a foot on a man's knee for just a moment, then removing it in a flash of perfectly formed calf.

Faster and faster she danced, the accompaniment of the guitar growing more insistent, more demanding with each moment.

The flamenco continued for what seemed an eternity. Therese was infatuation, obsession, forbidden. Every man in that saloon wanted her, yet every man knew, somehow, they could never have her.

Therese finally reached the Rangers. The guitar and her castanets merged in one blazing crescendo, and then abruptly stopped. Therese threw herself on her back across Jim's lap, one arm around his neck. She stared into his eyes with a fiery passion, her ardor so intense it seemed to set his very being aflame. There was no sound except for the hushed breaths of the audience.

Slowly, deliberately, Therese pulled Jim's head lower, pressing his lips to hers. She held him there, locked in a long, lingering kiss.

Finally, she released him.

"*Gracias, mi Corazon!*" she exclaimed, in a voice so tempting no man could resist.

"*De . . . de nada, Senorita,*" was all Jim could stammer out.

Therese rose from the Ranger's lap, draped her scarf around his shoulders and pulled him to her, kissed him full on the lips once again, then, bowing to the audience, worked her way back to the stage. A moment later she disappeared, while wild applause, raucous whistles and catcalls rocked the saloon.

Smoky waved his hand in front of Jim's face while his partner stared after the dancer. "Jim. You still breathin', pard?"

"Yeah, Smoke," Jim half-whispered. His lips were smeared with Therese's lipstick. "How about Eric?"

"Seems to be."

Bill Handy walked up to the trio.

"Well, what did you think of my dancer?"

"Incredible," Smoky said.

"Fantastic," Jim echoed.

"What about you, son?" the saloonkeeper asked Eric.

"She can't be real," Eric whispered.

"I assure you she is. And she'll be back later for another performance."

"We stayin' for that, Jim?" Smoky questioned.

"We need to get an early start," Jim answered. "But I reckon we'll stick around here a bit longer."

"In that case why don't we resume our card game?" said Piccirillo.

"Not me. The cards just aren't fallin' for me tonight," Jim said. "But I'm sure my pards would like to play a bit more. I'll just watch."

"Uh-uh. Me neither," Smoky added. "I'm just gonna head over to the bar and have a couple more drinks."

"I reckon that leaves me," Eric said. "I wouldn't mind playing a bit longer."

"Then let's get down to business," Piccirillo replied.

Hank McCarthy and Don Strothers also resumed the game. After several hands Eric's luck had changed for the worse. He had lost all of his winnings, plus considerably more. The youngster became tenser with each lost pot. He was considerably relieved when he threw three like cards on the table.

"Three jacks. Try and beat that," he said smiling.

"Good cards, kid. But not good enough," Piccirillo answered. He tossed down three kings. "I win again."

Eric leapt to his feet, knocking his chair over.

"You cheated, Mister!" he yelled, and grabbed for his gun.

The boy halted with his gun only half out of leather. A short-barreled revolver had slid from inside Piccirillo's shirtsleeve and appeared in his hand so quickly its movement was a blur. The gambler stood with the weapon pointed directly at Eric's nose, less than a foot away.

"I didn't cheat. Go ahead and try for that gun of yours if you want to die right here, kid."

Smoky had turned from the bar. Jim was half-out of his chair. Both Rangers were helpless, knowing there was no chance to stop Eric's death if he went for his six-gun.

"All right. You win," Eric stuttered. "But I still say you're a cheat."

"What you think doesn't matter to me. Just get out of here. And don't show your face in here again." Piccirillo slid the gun back in his sleeve and sat down.

Jim glared at the gambler, his blue eyes cold and deadly. "Give the kid his money back," he said. "And don't try pullin' that sleeve gun on me, unless you want a slug in your guts. I knew you had a weapon on you somewhere, but I just couldn't figure out where. I've seen sleeve guns before, but sure couldn't spot yours. Right clever hidin' your pistol so well."

Piccirillo snarled a vicious oath before he replied. "What'd you say, Ranger? I don't believe I heard you correctly."

"You heard me all right. I dunno whether you cheated or not, but you took advantage of a boy here tonight, a boy who's had enough trouble over the past few weeks. Give him his money back or I take it out of your hide."

Piccirillo stiffened, and then his face relaxed in an unctuous smile. "All right. I reckon it ain't worth takin' on a couple of Rangers for a few measly *pesos*. Here you go, kid."

Piccirillo pulled a handful of coins and bills from his pocket and tossed them on the table. Eric gathered them up and stuffed the money in his shirt pocket.

"I figure we've had enough excitement for the night. Let's get outta here," Jim said. Sweat was beading his forehead, and he was shivering. He turned toward the door.

"Look out, Jim!" Eric shouted.

Jim whirled and pulled his gun, too late. A bullet from Piccirillo's pistol put a hole through the loose fabric of his shirt as it burned between his side and upper arm. Jim's return shot shattered the gambler's right wrist. Piccirillo's short-barreled revolver spun from his hand.

At the same time, Eric pulled his gun and fired

165

twice, both his slugs tearing into Piccirillo's side, the first glancing off a rib to angle upward through his stomach, the second plowing through a lung and into his heart. The gambler took two tentative steps, eyes glazing. He muttered a curse, and fell onto the table. The table collapsed under his weight, chips, cards, and glasses scattering. Piccirillo rolled onto his back, sighed deeply, and shuddered. With one long gasp the life left him. Jim kicked the gun away from the gambler's body.

Smoky rushed up to his partner. "Jim! You all right?"

Jim glanced at the hole in the armpit of his shirt. "I'm okay. It was darn close, though."

"Too dang close," said Smoky.

"Thanks for savin' my hide, kid," Jim said to Eric.

"He was gonna shoot you in the back. I couldn't let him," Eric replied. The boy was clearly upset at killing his first man.

"I'm certainly glad." Jim shook his head. "I never expected him to try a stunt like that. Dunno what I was thinkin' turnin' my back on him."

Jim reloaded his Peacemaker, slid it back in its holster, and pitched to his face.

Jim awoke in a soft bed in an unfamiliar room. Someone had removed his shirt, bandanna, boots, socks, and gun belt. He opened his eyes to find Therese Marchitto gazing down at him. Worry showed in her dark eyes. Even in the dim light, scrubbed clean of makeup, she still was spectacular.

"I must've been shot worse'n I thought." Jim grinned at the dancer. "Appears like I've died and gone to heaven."

"You might wish so, but you are only in my bedroom," she softly replied.

"You mean this ain't heaven, doggone it?" Jim grinned. "Sure seems like it. I am lookin' at an angel, after all."

"Not at all, on both counts. And you haven't been shot at all, at least not tonight." Therese retorted.

"Then what am I doing here? And where are my pardners?"

"I heard the gunshots in the saloon. I came from my dressing room just as you fainted. I had you brought here," Therese explained.

"Your partners were here, but they have gone for the night to get their rest. They will return later this morning."

"But why'd you bring me here? You don't know me."

"You are quite ill. The doctor here has no beds at his office. You would have had to stay at the hotel, which isn't fit for a swine. And there would have been no one to tend to you. So I brought you to my home and made the doctor come here for his examination."

"But since I wasn't shot what did he say is wrong with me?"

"You have a fever. In addition, you have a bullet wound to your back that was partially healed, but has become infected. And you have quite a number of bruises on your body. The doctor says you need rest."

"I can't," Jim protested. "I have to be on the trail at sunup."

"You won't be going anywhere for at least two days," Therese answered.

"I don't have one day to waste, let alone two."

"You do not have any choice in the matter," Therese said. "There will be no traveling by anyone for at least a day or more in any event. It is storming—a rainstorm that promises to be a terrible deluge. Already the roads are becoming impassable."

As if to emphasize the dancer's words, a rumble of thunder echoed through the room.

"All right, say I am stuck here. That still doesn't explain why you brought me, a stranger, here to your place."

"Do you think I chose you of all those men in the saloon by accident, Ranger? I assure you I did not."

"How'd you know I'm a Ranger?" Jim demanded.

"Bill Handy told me. He tells me everything."

"I see. But that still doesn't explain why I'm here in your bed. Unless you've got cards you're not showin', you didn't pick me out of that crowd in the Frog Rock then take me home because I'm a Texas Ranger."

"You're right. I chose you out of all those men because I love *hombres* with *rubio* hair and *azul* eyes." Therese laughed. "Of course, I never expected to have you as a guest in my home."

"I have to admit I was pretty surprised when I woke up. I guess if I'm gonna be laid up for a couple of days I could do worse than here."

"Is that supposed to be a compliment?"

"It was, but I guess it didn't come out that way."

"Then I shall take it for one," Therese answered. "Now, it is very early in the morning. You should get more rest. I'll brew some tea. That will help you sleep."

"Please don't put yourself out, ma'am."

"Ma'am?" Therese laughed. "I can't recall the last time someone called me 'ma'am.' That sounds so old. Please, my name is Therese. And it's no trouble at all to make tea for a handsome man. You just stay there. I will be back shortly."

"Whatever you say . . . Therese. And my name's Jim."

Therese went to the kitchen. Jim could hear her

putting a kettle on the stove. Ten minutes later she returned with a silver tray holding a china teapot, two cups and saucers. She placed the tray on a bedside table.

"I told you this wouldn't take long, Jim. Would you like sugar with your tea?"

Jim sat up, pulling the covers to his chin to keep his naked upper torso covered. "Two lumps, please," he answered.

Therese poured two cups full of the steaming liquid and passed one to the Ranger. Jim took a sip, then a good swallow. The tea spread soothing warmth through his worn-out body.

"That does taste mighty good," he said smiling. "Thank you."

"I told you so." Therese smiled back, her dazzling white teeth seemed to light up the room. "Jim, it would be much easier for you to balance your cup if you didn't attempt to keep holding those sheets up to your shoulders."

"I always try to stay decent in the presence of a lady."

"You needn't worry about that. Don't forget, I helped bring you here and get you undressed. There's nothing left to hide or to be ashamed of. Besides, you're still wearing your Levis."

Jim blushed, but did let the covers slide down to his waist.

"That's better," Therese declared. "Once we finish our tea, I'll leave you to relax some more.

Remember, the more you rest, the faster you will be able to resume your journey."

"I reckon that's good advice."

Jim drank two more cups of tea before he settled back with a sigh. As Therese had promised, he was again sleepy, his body suffused with a delicious warmth.

"I think I'm gonna drift off again. Good night, Therese."

"Good night, Jim."

Therese leaned over and kissed him on the cheek, her hand brushing lightly against Jim's bare shoulder. "Sleep well."

Jim spent most of the next day sleeping and regaining some of his strength. Smoky, Eric, and Sheriff Pierce stopped by for a brief visit, eating dinner with their recuperating *compadre*. The rainstorm continued, so intense it had even prevented Eric from completing his journey home.

After they left, the town physician returned to check Jim once again. He pronounced the Ranger's fever rapidly falling, and declared him to be recovering far more quickly than he had expected.

After supper Therese returned with a tray holding a pitcher of warm water, a basin, soap, washcloth, towel, bandages, and medicines.

"It's time to redress and rebandage the wound

to your back," she said to Jim. "I also have a poultice for your chest. Dr. Morris says that will help reduce your fever. And I thought you might like to wash up a bit. I can also find a razor if you'd like to shave. I could even trim your hair."

Jim ran his hand over the thick blonde whiskers covering his jaw. "I reckon just washin' up'll do for now."

Therese pulled the covers to the bottom of the bed. "Whatever you wish. We'll start with your back. Please turn onto your stomach."

Jim complied, rolling onto his belly.

"This is going to hurt a bit," Therese warned.

Jim winced when she pulled the bandage from his back.

"What I have to do now will probably feel even worse," she said.

Jim jerked when Therese pressed hard on both sides of the bullet hole, expelling pus from the inflamed wound. The pus soon was replaced by blood. Therese dabbed a cloth to staunch the flow.

"I know that was uncomfortable, but it had to be done," she explained. "That wound really is looking much better. It's draining quite well. I'll clean it thoroughly and wash your back before I replace the bandages."

"It wasn't all that awful," Jim reassured her.

"If you say so, Jim, but I know better."

Therese took the washcloth, soaked it in the

warm water and wet Jim's back. Taking the damp cloth and the bar of soap, she worked up lather, and then began gently scrubbing the Ranger's back.

"You have a strong muscular back," she said as she worked her fingers down his backbone. "And a good, straight, spine."

Jim shifted uncomfortably. His face was flushed, and not from any fever or infected bullet wound.

Finished washing his back, Therese carefully dried it. "I'm going to redress and rebandage your injury now." It took her only a few moments to coat Jim's wound and cover it with a fresh bandage.

"Now I need you to turn onto your back."

Once again, Jim complied with her request. Despite himself, he found he was staring at the dancer. Trying to get his thoughts off the woman, he asked her the question he'd been pondering since she first picked him out of the crowded saloon.

"Therese, you knew I was a Texas Ranger before I ever walked into the Frog Rock, didn't you?"

"That's right," she admitted.

"And that's the reason you chose me that night?"

"Again, you are correct."

"But why? And don't try and tell me it's just

because you like men with blonde hair and blue eyes."

"That's the only reason," Therese insisted.

"I'm not convinced. Do you want to keep me from goin' after Reese Macklin? Were you ever his gal, or does he have some kind of claim on you?"

Therese hesitated before replying.

"Yes and no. Reese Macklin and I had some good times, but that's all. I found out what he was quite some time back. He beat me when I refused to let him have his way with me. When I threw him out, he threatened to kill me. I think later he realized if he ever hurt me the entire county would hunt him down. Besides, I carry this."

Therese lifted her skirt, revealing her well-formed calf, and pulled a long, thin-bladed knife from her garter. Her dark eyes flashed with anger.

"If Reese Macklin ever comes near me again, I will geld him."

"Ouch!" Jim winced. He managed a weak smile. "That still doesn't explain the Frog Rock."

"I wanted to get your attention, in hopes to speak with you privately later that evening. Of course those plans were ruined by the gunfight."

"Well, you've got your chance now."

"I wanted to warn you about Reese. He's a very dangerous man."

"I know that," Jim replied.

"But you don't know he also has some powerful

friends. Friends who have connections in Austin."

"That doesn't matter. I'm going to hunt down Reese Macklin and his men. Pure and simple."

"That is what I had hoped you would say," she replied. "Sheriff Pierce and your partner told me what Reese and his men did to your wife and boy, and that you had vowed revenge on them. Now I can tell you the truth. I want Reese Macklin gunned down like the cur he is."

She leaned close and whispered. Her lips brushed Jim's cheek. "Will you do that for me, Lieutenant?"

"You didn't need to bother going to all that trouble, not that it wasn't enjoyable," Jim answered. "Reese Macklin and the rest of his outfit are dead men."

"That is what I wanted to hear. But please be careful. Reese thinks he is invincible because of his connections. And he will stop at nothing to get what he wants." Therese sighed. "Now please, let me finish bathing you before you catch your death of pneumonia."

Therese took the washcloth and soap. She began lathering Jim's chest, running her hands through its covering of thick blonde hair.

"You've been hurt quite a few times," she noted, referring to the scars Jim's body carried.

"I reckon." Jim shrugged. "Comes with the territory."

"Try to hold still," she asked.

"I'll do my best," he answered.

Despite his fierce loyalty to Julia, Jim was still a man, a man alone in a bedroom with a gorgeous woman. Regardless of his determination to remain faithful, his blood was racing and pulse pounding.

"You need to lift your left arm just a bit," Therese requested. "You do have a slight bullet burn from Piccirillo's shot under it, and I need to make sure I clean that thoroughly. You don't want to have another wound become infected."

Jim moved his arm away from his ribs. When Therese ran the washcloth over the bullet crease and under his armpit, he laughed involuntarily.

"Jim?"

"I'm sorry. I can't help it. I'm really ticklish on my sides," he explained.

"That's something I never would have expected from you, Jim."

Therese resumed washing the Ranger's torso, gently massaging as she worked her way lower, now soaping his belly.

Therese leaned over him, scrubbing his skin. Her long black hair drifted over Jim's chest. Her hands were now kneading his lower abdomen. Unconsciously she began tracing the rim of Jim's bellybutton.

Jim had been trying to fight off the stirrings of his body as Therese worked on him. However, the last time he and Julia had made love was two nights before the attack on the JB Bar. Now, with the tantalizing Therese Marchitto massaging his flat belly, urges too powerful to resist were beginning to rouse in his groin. He groaned.

"Therese."

The dancer appeared not to hear him. She continued to rub her soapy hand across his belly.

"Therese!" Jim repeated, louder.

"What is it?"

"I think you'd better stop. I'll finish washing myself."

Therese looked down and jerked her hand away from Jim's beltline.

"Jim, I'm so embarrassed," she stammered. "I didn't realize what was happening. I hope you understand that is not the kind of woman I am. I had no intention of . . . of . . ."

Jim put a finger to her lips.

"Shh. I'm sure you're not, and you didn't," he assured her. "Just like I'm a married man, and would never be unfaithful to Julia. Nonetheless, this is far too tempting a situation. We need to make sure things don't get out of hand before it's too late and we do something we'll both regret."

"For the rest of our lives," Therese concluded. "I was just about done anyway, thank goodness. Here's the towel. You can dry yourself. While you do that, I will prepare that poultice for your chest."

"I think perhaps you might want to let me apply that poultice on my own," Jim noted.

"Nonsense! You could never apply it properly," Therese replied. "Besides, that poultice smells so horrible it will stifle any thoughts of romance. Now you dry yourself while I get it ready."

Jim watched Therese as she left the room. He sat up, drying himself vigorously. Those past few moments with the incredibly alluring dancer were the closest he had ever come to being unfaithful to his wife and, hopefully, closer than he ever would again.

Jim finished toweling himself off and dropped back on his pillows with a sigh.

A few moments later Therese returned, carrying a bowl filled with a steaming, foul-smelling substance.

"Whoa! What is that stuff?" Jim exclaimed.

"It's Doctor Morris's own concoction," Therese replied with a laugh. She sniffed at the bowl, her nose wrinkling. "And as I said, this odor will drive any thoughts of love right out of your head."

"Boy howdy, that's for certain," Jim agreed. "Smells worse'n a saloon full of cowboys after a month on the trail and smokin' *peso* cigars."

"You've got it just about right," Therese concurred. "But Doctor Morris insists it's the cure for your fever. So just hold your nose while I plaster this over your chest."

Therese sat alongside Jim's bed to apply the thick, pungent brew over his chest.

"I figure you wasted your time scrubbin' me down before puttin' this stuff on me," Jim complained.

"You needed to wash in any event, and I'm just about finished. Does it seem to be working?"

"I dunno. The stink alone might be knockin' me out." Jim grinned. "But yeah, it seems to be doin' somethin'."

"Then it's working. That's good. You will sleep soundly all night and wake up refreshed," Therese said.

She finished spreading the poultice over Jim's chest. "Now unless there's anything else you need I'm going to get some rest myself," she said. "I have to go back to work tomorrow."

"There's just one thing," Jim answered.

"What's that?"

"This."

Jim dipped his fingers into the poultice covering his chest, taking some to wipe it on the tip of Therese's nose and on her chest, just above her cleavage.

"If I've gotta smell this bad, it's only fair that you do too, lady." He laughed. "Besides, if Reese Macklin somehow gets me before I get him, the smell of this stuff will keep him away from you."

"And I thought you were an honorable man," Therese said.

"Good night, Lieutenant Blawcyzk."

"G'night, Therese Marchitto."

Once Therese had left, Jim recited his evening prayers while the heat from the poultice suffused his body. He soon fell into a deep, peaceful sleep. He awakened sometime in the pre-dawn hours to a soft murmuring.

Jim rolled from his bed, opened the door, and stepped into the hallway. The soft voice was coming from a room down the hall. Quietly, Jim padded barefoot down the corridor. He stopped when he reached the source of the sound.

Therese, her head covered by a black lace veil, was kneeling in front of a small candle-lit shrine to Our Lady of Guadalupe. She had a set of rosary beads in her right hand. The murmuring which had awakened Jim was Therese praying.

Jim went back to his room, retrieved his shirt, and slipped into it. He returned to where Therese had her head bowed in prayer and knelt beside her. Therese gave him a slight smile, and resumed her rosary.

Jim folded his hands and bowed his head. Side by side the rugged Texas Ranger and the hardened saloon entertainer whispered their prayers, comforted by the presence of the Blessed Virgin.

Chapter 16

Two mornings later Jim was raring to go. The rain had stopped, and the Rangers and Eric hit the trail before sunrise. The roads were still muddy and slick, so the going was slow and tedious. By late afternoon, they reached the fork in the trail which led to the Rocking E, the Esposito ranch.

"You're certain you don't want us to ride along with you until you reach home, Eric?" Jim asked.

"I'll be fine," the youngster replied. "Besides, you don't want to waste any more time catchin' up to Reese Macklin. It's still a three-hour ride to my place. You'd end up losin' another whole day if you came along."

"All right. I just want to thank you again for savin' my hide back there in Bartlett, son," Jim said. "And you'll get a message from Austin when you can pick up your broncs."

"You got back our stolen horses and are goin' after the men who shot my dad, so you're doin' just as much for me," Eric responded.

"Kid, if you ever want to join the Texas Rangers, just give Captain Trumbull our names," Smoky added. "You're a man to ride the river with."

"I appreciate that, Smoky. But I reckon this is *adios* for now."

"You take care, Eric. *Vaya con Dios*," Jim said.

Eric turned his blue roan and loped out of sight.

"Jim, we gonna try and make Buckholts today?" asked Smoky.

"No, we'd have to travel half the night. I figure to find a place to hole up just before sundown, then hit the trail again before first light. That should put us in Buckholts by early morning. We'll grab some breakfast, pick up what information we can, then head out after Macklin."

"Good idea about the grub. I never did hanker to die on an empty belly," Smoky said. He took a deep drag on his cigarette.

"The only dyin' will be done by Macklin and his outfit, Smoky. Bet a hat on it."

The pair rode mostly in silence for the next two hours, until they found a campsite by a small pond. They cared for their horses, ate a quick supper, and rolled up in their blankets.

The dawn mist still shrouded the ground when Jim and Smoky rode into Buckholts the next morning.

"Somethin' sure smells good in this town," said Smoky. "It's makin' me even hungrier than I already was."

"Well, it shouldn't be too hard to find the source," Jim said. "This place ain't too big."

Buckholts was a small hamlet, barely large enough to be called a town. There wasn't even a livery stable in sight, just a common corral at the far end of its short main street. And so far no one was stirring.

"There's the place we want," Jim said. He pointed to a small building with "Whitney Bakery and Café" lettered over its door.

"Let's put up the horses and head on over there," said Smoky.

Sizzle and Soot were unsaddled, rubbed down, and turned loose in the empty corral. As always, Sizzle insisted on his peppermint. Once Sizzle had eaten his treat, he and Soot ducked their noses to suck up water from the trough, while their riders forked hay stored in a lean-to over the fence for them.

Satisfied their horses were settled, the Rangers headed for the bakery. They entered and took seats at a small counter.

"I'll be right with you," a voice called from the back room. A moment later the voice's owner stepped from the room. He was tall, with thinning black hair and dark eyes. He carried a tray of hot, freshly-made doughnuts. Almost as much powdered sugar coated the man's deep blue shirt and his apron as the doughnuts.

"What can I do for you gentlemen?" he asked.

Smoky's eyes grew wide at the sight of the doughnuts. "You can set that tray right here in front of me," he said, "along with a pot of black coffee."

"You want all these doughnuts?" was the baker's incredulous response.

"Well, I might let my pardner have a few, but I can't remember the last time I had hot doughnuts. Just leave the tray."

"Whatever you say, gents. You're the customers. I'm Pete, the owner of this bakery."

"Well, if your doughnuts taste as good as they smell, you must do a heckuva business," Jim answered.

Smoky already had half a doughnut stuffed in his mouth, powdered sugar sprinkling his whiskers. "They do, Jim. Try 'em," he mumbled, and swallowed.

"Wonderful doughnuts, Pete. I'm Jim. My pard here's Smoky."

Pete lifted a pot of steaming coffee from the stove and two mugs from a shelf. He placed these in front of the Rangers and filled both.

"There's plenty more where that came from. Doughnuts too," he said.

"Thanks," Jim replied.

"I haven't seen you boys before. What brings you to these parts?" Pete asked.

"We're lookin' for Reese Macklin. You know where we might find him?"

Pete jerked the coffeepot from the counter.

"You're not lookin' to join up with that bunch of renegades, are you? Because if you are, then get out of my shop! Right now! And don't think of settin' foot inside my place again."

"Whoa. Easy, Pete. We're not lookin' to ride with Macklin."

Jim dug in his shirt pocket, pulled out his Ranger badge, and pinned it to his vest. "We're lookin' to bring that whole bunch in, belly-down over their saddles."

"Well, we're gonna bring 'em in, anyway," Smoky said pulling out his badge and pinning it to his vest. "Dead or alive. Which way depends on how much of a fight they put up."

Pete stared at the silver stars on silver circles glittering on the men's vests. "You're Texas Rangers?"

"That's right. Rangers Jim Blawcyzk and Smoky McCue." Jim said.

"Well, I'm sure glad to see the two of you," Pete declared. "Reese Macklin and his bunch have been ridin' roughshod over everyone in these parts for far too long. It's about time someone settles their hash."

"Speakin' of hash, Pete, you wouldn't by chance have any, would you?" Smoky requested.

"For you Rangers, sure. Anything you want. Comin' right up."

Pete disappeared into the kitchen. Soon the banging of pots and pans and the sizzling of frying meat, potatoes, and eggs filled the small café.

Smoky poured himself another mug of coffee,

grabbed another doughnut, then rolled and lighted a quirly. "I don't think our friend Pete cares much for Reese Macklin," he observed.

"I think that's pretty plain," Jim replied.

Pete returned with a heaping plate of hash.

"Just pile it on," Smoky requested.

"How about you, Jim?" Pete asked.

"None for me, thanks," Jim answered. "These doughnuts'll do just fine."

"He's only eaten a dozen and a half so far," Smoky pointed out.

Once the Rangers finished their meal, they lingered for a few minutes over final mugs of coffee. A few more customers had entered the shop, nodded at the Rangers, then hastened to the far side of the room.

"Looks like folks are afraid to get too near us," Smoky said.

"That's cause if Reese Macklin or any of his boys happen to spot you there'll be a shootin' scrape. You can count on that," Pete said.

"Pete, to get back to my original question, where is Macklin's place?" Jim again asked.

"It's just about two miles east of town. A small ranch, not in bad shape considering a mess of owlhoots live there. No sign, but there's a big double-trunked live oak at the gate. You can't miss that tree. The buildings are about a quarter-mile after you turn in."

"You have any idea whether Macklin's there

right now? And how many men are with him?"

"He should be, although with Macklin there's no guarantee. You never can tell when he might head out. He's usually got anywhere from six to eight men workin' for him."

"*Gracias*," Jim replied. "Time to get ridin'. Pete, those doughnuts were the best I've ever tasted, bar none. What do we owe you?"

"Taking care of Reese Macklin and his bunch will be payment enough. But there are still four doughnuts on your plate. Are you sure twenty were enough for you two?"

"I could probably squeeze in a few more," Smoky said laughing.

Jim and Smoky pushed up from their chairs. Pete bagged the remaining doughnuts and handed them to Jim.

"I want to wish the both of you good luck. But be careful. Reese Macklin's a dangerous man," Pete advised.

Jim's voice was dead calm when he replied. "Not half as dangerous as I'll be when I finally catch up with him."

"I believe that, Ranger," the bakery owner said. "And you be sure and stop back here once your work is finished."

"We'll do that," Jim promised. "*Adios*, Pete."

They emerged from the bakery to hear the snorts and squeals of a horse coming from the corral.

"That's Sizzle!" Jim hollered. He jerked his Colt and broke into a run, Smoky hard on his heels.

Inside the corral, a rough-looking cowboy sat on a saddled and bridled Sizzle. The horse had his ears pinned back and his feet planted deep in the soil. Despite the rider's jabbing spurs into the big paint's flanks and whipping the reins across his neck, the horse refused to move. Even when the horse thief yanked back on the reins and slapped them across the gelding's rump, Sizzle refused to move forward. He stood still, except for one or two rearward steps when the pressure on the bit became too much to bear. Finally, Sizzle dropped to his knees, and rolled onto his side. The cursing horse thief barely leapt from the saddle in time to avoid being crushed under twelve hundred pounds of horseflesh.

"Step away from that horse, Mister!" Jim snarled.

The outlaw grabbed for his gun.

Jim and Smoky fired at the same moment, Smoky's bullet taking the horse thief in his stomach, Jim's in his right hip. The man crumpled. The Rangers ducked under the fence and into the corral. Sizzle trotted up to Jim and nuzzled his neck.

"In a minute, Siz," Jim said.

Smoky rolled the badly wounded outlaw onto

his back and wrenched the gun from his hand. "He's about done for, Jim," he said.

"You tried stealin' my horse, and you're payin' for it," Jim said.

"Made a mistake. Stubborn cayuse. Just about the worst one . . . I've ever come across," the dying man muttered. "Only one worse was a horse back in San Leanna. Like to have killed me. Had to shoot him."

"You're Clete King!" Jim exclaimed. "The no-good coyote that tried to steal my horse and ended up cripplin' him."

He rammed the barrel of his Colt against King's forehead.

"Jim Blawcyzk!" King exclaimed. "But, but it can't be you. We left you lyin' dead."

"I'm not dead, King, and every man in Macklin's outfit is gonna pay for that mistake." Jim thumbed back the hammer of his Colt.

"Don't do it, Jim," Smoky said. "He's already done for."

Jim eased down the hammer and slipped the Colt into its holster. "I know that," he answered. "Besides, he'll die a lot slower this way. And even dyin' gut-shot's better'n he deserves. C'mon, Smoke, let's get outta here."

Ignoring the curious crowd gathering outside the corral, the Rangers left the renegade lying there in a puddle of blood. Jim checked over Sizzle while Smoky saddled Soot. Satisfied the horse was not injured, Jim opened the sack of doughnuts and placed one on the palm of his hand.

"I saved these for you, Siz. Maybe they'll make up a bit for what that *hombre* did to you."

Sizzle snatched the doughnut from Jim's hand and nosed the sack for more.

"I guess you like 'em as much as I do," Jim said laughing. He gave the paint the remaining pastries.

"I figure you learned one thing today, Jim," Smoky remarked as he tightened his cinches.

"What's that?"

"Sizzle there's just like Sam. He ain't ever gonna be stolen. That bronc's never leavin' your side, pardner."

"I guess you're right, Smoke. Stealin' him has been tried twice, and twice it didn't work." He patted the big gelding's shoulder. "Reckon I'm stuck with you, pal," he said.

Jim and Smoky climbed into their saddles. Two minutes later, they were galloping out of Buckholts.

Chapter 17

Two miles east of town, Smoky reined Soot to a halt. He pointed ahead to a tremendous double-trunked live oak. "That has to be the oak tree Pete described, Jim."

"It's gotta be. There sure ain't gonna be another one like it in these parts. Better check our weapons."

Jim pulled his Peacemaker from its holster, checked the action, and replaced it. He did the same with his Winchester.

After checking his guns, Smoky hooked a leg over his saddlehorn. He pulled the makings from his vest pocket and began to build a quirly. "How do you want to handle this?" he asked.

"I figure we'll just ride on in there and take that bunch," Jim replied.

Smoky rolled the paper and licked it to seal the edges. He stuck the cigarette between his lips, lit it, and took a deep drag before answering. "Macklin and his men might not be all that cooperative. It's not gonna be easy roustin' them outta there, but I guess that's as good a plan as any. You reckon there'll be guards posted?"

"I doubt it. From what everyone's said, Macklin's got folks around here buffaloed. He's not worried about any lawmen ridin' up on his place."

Jim paused and grinned.

"Besides, Macklin and his whole outfit think I'm dead, remember?"

Smoky gave a rueful chuckle. "If any of 'em get the drop on us before we get in there you will be. Both of us, for that matter. Maybe we'll get lucky and surprise 'em. How many do you think we'll be up against?"

"Well, if Pete's estimate was right, Macklin had eight men in his outfit, includin' himself. My boy killed one of 'em, and we just downed Clete King. So that should leave six."

"Unless Macklin's hired more riders in the meantime," Smoky pursed his lips inhaling deeply off his quirly and let the smoke drift out of his nostrils.

"He most likely has, but there's only one way to find out," Jim answered.

"I reckon you're right. Well, let's get this over with." Smoky took one last pull on his cigarette, crushed out the butt on his saddlehorn, then tossed it aside.

"I reckon we'd best leave the horses here and go in the rest of the way on foot," Jim said. He swung out of his saddle and tied Sizzle to a scrubby juniper. Smoky did likewise with Soot.

Jim pulled his rifle from its scabbard, then dug a peppermint from his hip pocket and gave it to his horse. "You wait here until I get back," he ordered the paint. "And behave yourself."

Sizzle whickered a soft response.

"You ready, Smoke?" Jim asked.

Smoky jacked the lever of his Winchester and spat on the ground. "I thought you'd never ask," he said, a lopsided grin crossing his face.

Rifles at the ready, crouching low and running, they headed for the confrontation with Reese Macklin and his men. They reached the fence surrounding the buildings unchallenged, and dove to their bellies behind its meager shelter.

"Looks like they're all in the house," Smoky muttered.

"No, they sure aren't," Jim replied. "Look!"

Eight men leading saddled horses emerged from the barn.

Jim leapt to his feet.

"Reese Macklin! Texas Rangers! You're all under arrest!"

"Jim! Are you loco? Get down!" Smoky yelled.

Macklin and his men stared in disbelief for just one moment, seeing the man they'd thought left dead with a bullet in his back and another in his brain standing there with a leveled rifle.

"Blawcyzk!" Macklin shouted, then grabbed for his gun.

"Too late!" Smoky exclaimed. He fired his Winchester, putting a bullet into one outlaw's chest and spinning him to the dirt.

Jim aimed just above Macklin's belt buckle, but when he fired Macklin's frightened horse pulled him aside. The bullet ripped through the stomach of another of the renegades. The man jackknifed and went down, trampled under the milling, panicked horses. The yard erupted in a maelstrom of flying lead, screaming men, and terrified horses.

Smoky grunted when a bullet tore along his ribs, but his return shot put a slug through the neck of the man who'd hit him. The outlaw dropped his pistol and grabbed his throat, trying in vain to stem the blood pumping from his severed jugular.

Jim's second shot punctured the shoulder of one of the three remaining men. Instantly Reese Macklin and Bob Perdue, the only other unwounded man, dropped their guns to the ground and lifted their hands in the air.

"We've had enough!" Macklin screamed.

"You might've had enough, but I'm not finished with you yet, Macklin!" Jim spat out the words. "Not after what you did to my wife and kid!"

Smoky covered Perdue and the wounded man, who lay clutching his bullet-punctured shoulder. "Don't even wiggle or I'll put a slug clean through you," he warned.

Jim stalked up to Macklin and jabbed the outlaw in his belly with the barrel of his Winchester, then swept Macklin's hat off his head, revealing his thatch of sandy hair. New growth had not yet completely filled in where Julia had ripped a chunk from the outlaw's scalp. Jim dug in his pocket, pulled out the hank of hair and piece of fabric he'd carried for these many days and miles, and threw them at Macklin's feet.

"I took that hair out of my wife's hand, Macklin! Your hair! You're the one who beat and raped my wife. Don't try and deny it. Now the only decision I have today is how slow I want you to die. But you are gonna die!"

"I ain't gonna deny it," Macklin replied.

"That's good, because it wouldn't matter if you did," Jim answered.

"Why deny it? I enjoyed havin' her too much." Macklin taunted. "I just wish I'd known you were still alive that day. I would have let you watch."

Furious, Jim reversed his Winchester and drove the butt into the pit of Macklin's stomach. The outlaw doubled over in pain, defiance still blazing in his pale blue eyes.

"Go ahead and kill me," Macklin said gasping for breath. "But I guarantee you'll regret it."

Jim aimed his rifle just below Macklin's belt buckle and levered a shell into the chamber.

"Don't do it, Jim," Smoky said. "If you kill him, you'll be just as bad as he is. You don't want that. It's not worth throwin' away everything you've stood for on the likes of Macklin."

"That doesn't matter, Smoke. Not after what he did to Julia."

"It does, Jim." Smoky reached out and touched his pardner on the arm. "You'd better think of Julia and Charlie. No matter what these side-winders did to them, they sure wouldn't want you to turn into a cold-blooded murderer on their account. Think what that would do to them. Especially if you ended up gettin' yourself hung for killin' this sorry s.o.b."

Jim stood there for a long moment, conflicting emotions etched on his face. He still held the rifle aimed at Macklin's belly, but the Winchester's barrel was shaking. Finally, Jim lowered the rifle.

"All right. You're talkin' sense, Smoke. I can't just gun him down. So I guess we'll have to make this a fair fight, man to man. Besides, I'll get a lot more satisfaction takin' him apart with my fists."

He laid his Winchester aside, then unbuckled his gunbelt and dropped it next to the rifle. "Smoke, you stay out of this," he ordered.

"It's your play, pardner."

"Same goes for you," Smoky said to Perdue and the wounded man.

"I'm done with this, Ranger," Perdue replied.

"And I'm hurtin' too much," said the wounded man.

"Okay, Macklin, I'm givin' you a chance," Jim said, his eyes like ice. He drove his fist into Macklin's stomach.

Macklin gasped, took a step back, and slammed a punch of his own into Jim's chest, staggering him. Macklin's following blow took Jim on the chin, spinning him to the ground.

Jim rolled onto his back. Macklin dove at him, and Jim sank both feet into Macklin's belly, flipping him over his head. Before Macklin could recover, Jim pounced on him, both men rolling over and over in the dirt. Macklin tossed Jim off, sprang to his feet, grabbed Jim's shirtfront, and pulled him upright. The shirt tore open at the chest, the right sleeve ripping off at the shoulder. Macklin smashed Jim in the mouth, then hard in the belly. Jim ducked his next punch to slam a solid left into Macklin's ribs.

The two men fought as only the bitterest of enemies could fight. There was nothing civilized about this battle. The combatants stood toe to toe, slugging it out. Rock-hard fists slammed into bellies, ribs, and jaws, blood splattering with each blow to the face.

Jim groaned when Macklin drove a knee into his crotch. He grabbed Macklin's neckerchief as he crumpled, dragging him down and half-choking him. Macklin tried to pull away, but Jim had a firm grip on the outlaw's bandanna and shirt. The shirt ripped apart as Macklin tried to break free.

Jim fought off the agony pulsing through his groin and lower belly. Hat on his back, he smashed several short, sharp blows into Macklin's gut. Macklin grunted, all the air driven out of his lungs. He rolled and forced himself to his hands and knees.

Jim struggled to his feet, standing with fist cocked over the stunned outlaw. Macklin had no strength left to rise. He held one hand to the back of his throbbing head. Both men gulped in great draughts of air.

"Had enough, Macklin?" Jim said spitting blood.

"Not quite," Macklin rasped. "I'm still gonna finish you, Ranger."

The outlaw attempted to push himself to his feet. Jim kicked him hard in the belly, flipping him onto his back. Macklin wrapped his arms around his middle, groaning.

"You've got that backwards, Macklin. I'm the one who's gonna finish you, once and for all."

"You . . . you ain't gonna kill me." Macklin gasped and tried to cover his bloody face.

"I can't think of one reason why I shouldn't," Jim said.

"I can. I'm the one man who can tell you who was really behind the raid on your ranch."

"Nice try, Macklin but you're just lyin' to save your sorry hide. Besides, what about your pardners over there? If there is such a person, one of them could tell me."

"Perdue and Haycroft don't know who ordered

that attack. Only me and Clete King met with that *hombre*. I ain't lyin', Ranger. Kill me and you'll never know who wanted you dead, your wife's and boy's lives ruined."

"Smoky, throw me my Colt," said Jim.

Smoky picked up Jim's Peacemaker and tossed it to him. Jim aimed the pistol directly at Macklin's middle.

"There are six bullets in this gun. Talk fast, Macklin. And if I don't like what you have to say I'll put all six slugs through your lousy guts."

"I said I'd tell. You recall a few years back there was a bad deal up in the Panhandle, involving the Texas Pacific Railroad?"

"You mean that scheme to wreck the railroad?"

"Yeah. The plan you and your pardners stopped."

"The men behind that are all dead or in prison," Jim said.

"They are. But Thaddeus Cox, that state senator you killed, had a brother, Justin. He's the man who wanted you dead for what you did to his kin. He's been bidin' his time all these years waitin' to get even."

"That doesn't make sense," said Smoky. "I've heard of Justin Cox. He's a wealthy man and a big wheel in state politics. He even has the governor's ear, from what I hear tell. Why would he risk all that to kill Jim?"

Macklin wiped the blood trickling from the corners of his mouth. "That's right. Cox is a powerful man over in east Texas. He's a commissioner in Leon County, and just about runs it. But hate's a powerful motive. You should know that, Ranger." Macklin shrugged his shoulders. "Me, I was just doin' what I was paid to do. There wasn't anythin' personal in it, except my natural dislike for all lawmen, so I was glad for the chance to kill one and get paid for it. But Cox's feelin's for Blawcyzk are pure poison."

"All right Macklin, suppose I believe your story," Jim said. "You've bought yourself some time, but you're still under arrest and headed for jail and probably the hangman's rope."

"You might put me in jail, but I won't stay there," Macklin said. "Cox'll spring me before long. That was part of our deal if anything went wrong. If you don't believe me check the top drawer in my desk inside the house. Everything's in writing. I made sure of that." The beaten outlaw started to sit up.

"Don't move, Macklin," Jim said. "Far as your boss goes, he won't be able to get you out if he's dead or in prison himself, which he will be once I'm done with him."

"I'm not worried about that." Macklin growled out an ugly laugh. "You'll never get to Cox. Besides his political influence, he has a small army of bodyguards. His chief man's a big feller, name of Mike Buckley. And his place outside of Leona is a fortress. You'll be dead before you get within a hundred yards of Cox."

"I wouldn't count on that," Jim answered. "I've got a friend in Leon County myself. Another Ranger, Jim Huggins. And he'll pull in one or two more Rangers if I ask him. I'm not worried, but Cox should be."

"We'll see. But once you're lyin' dead and I'm turned loose, maybe I'll go visit your widow again. That'd sure give me pleasure."

Enraged, Jim drove the toe of his boot into Macklin's groin. The outlaw screeched in anguish. "I might not kill you, Macklin, but that doesn't mean I can't fix you so you'll never again go near another woman," Jim ground his boot heel into Macklin's groin. Macklin curled up on his side, clutching his crotch and whimpering. Tears of pain streaked his cheeks.

"Easy, Jim, he's had enough," Smoky said.

"I reckon you're right, Smoke," Jim answered. "Besides, we'd better try and get to Cox before word gets back to him about what happened here."

"Not to mention, since I haven't reported in, Cap'n Trumbull's gotta have half the Rangers in Texas lookin' for both of us right now, so we'd better finish our business before one of 'em finds us." Smoky scratched his jaw. "What're we gonna do with these *hombres*?"

"We'll put 'em in the county jail at Cameron. I'm sure the sheriff there'll be glad to finally see them behind bars. We'll load up the bodies of the others and leave them with the sheriff too."

"I can't ride a horse. It'd just about kill me," Macklin whined.

"You'd best plan on it, unless you'd rather be roped belly-down over a saddle like your dead pards, or maybe you'd prefer walkin' or bein' dragged along by a rope," Jim said.

Smoky whirled at a sudden flicker of movement behind one of the house windows. He put a bullet through the top pane, shattering the glass. "Whoever's left in there, throw out your guns and come out with your hands up," he ordered.

The door opened, and two scantily clad women emerged from the house. One of them was weeping, the other cursing the Rangers. This one charged Smoky, and beat her fists on his chest. Jim shifted his gun from the pain paralyzed Macklin to cover Perdue and Haycroft.

Smoky grabbed the woman's wrists. "Whoa. Easy, honey!" he said.

"What have you done? You killed my man!" she screeched, then again hurled oaths at the lawmen.

"Settle down or I'll hogtie you and haul you to jail," said Smoky.

"You'd better listen to him, Lillie," the other woman said still sobbing.

"Linda Mae, they shot Monk," Lillie screamed. "Now what will I do?"

"I imagine you'll just keep on workin' at what you've been doin'," Smoky said still holding Lillie by both wrists.

"You'd best take your friend's advice and quiet down," Jim warned the woman. "I don't much care what you've been up to, or what you intend to do now. We'll leave you a couple of horses, so my advice is you ride back to town, since there's no reason for you to stay here."

"He's right, Lillie. There's nothing left for us here," Linda Mae said. "These Rangers could have made us walk back to town. At least they're not doing that. We'll survive like we always have."

"I guess you're right. They're not giving us a choice," Lillie replied. "All right, Ranger, you can let me go. We'll get out of your way."

Smoky released the woman. Lillie cursed both men ferociously, but headed for the barn along with her companion.

"I don't think they like us, Jim," Smoky said chuckling.

"I think that's an understatement," Jim answered. "Let's get movin'."

Leaving Smoky to guard the captives, Jim picked up the piece of Macklin's hair and shirt and headed to the house. It only took a moment for him to find the papers Macklin had indicated.

He quickly scanned them, and then shoved them inside his shirt. "Well, these prove he wasn't lyin'," he muttered, "and they should give me enough evidence to have Justin Cox put away for a long time, maybe the rest of his life."

Macklin, Perdue, and Haycroft were tied; Haycroft's wound bandaged. They were left waiting while the bodies of the other men were tied over their horses. Once that was completed, Smoky retrieved the Rangers' mounts. Sizzle whinnied when he spotted Jim, trotted up to him, and dropped his nose to Jim's hip pocket.

"Peppermint." Jim laughed and gave the horse his treat.

Smoky saddled the three remaining horses and led them to the waiting prisoners. "Mount up," he ordered the men.

Perdue climbed into the saddle of his roan. Smoky tied his wrists to the saddlehorn and ankles to the stirrups.

"I'm gonna need some help," Haycroft said.

Smoky helped the wounded man into the saddle and tied him in place.

Jim hauled Macklin to his feet and shoved him onto his horse. Macklin yelped, cringing in pain when he hit the saddle.

"I can't ride. Hurts too much," he choked out.

Jim rapped Macklin's temple with the butt of his Colt. Macklin moaned and slumped unconscious over his horse's neck.

"Won't hurt now," Jim said. He tied Macklin to his horse, and picked up the reins.

Jim climbed into his own saddle. Smoky had already mounted. Jim glanced at the blood staining the side of his partner's shirt. You need patchin' up?" he questioned.

"No. That slug just clipped me. The bleeding's already stopped. I'll take care of myself when we get to Cameron," Smoky answered.

"Then let's go." Jim heeled Sizzle into a lope.

Chapter 18

The Rangers stopped in Cameron long enough to drop off their prisoners and the dead outlaws, grab a quick bite, and rest and grain their horses. Since the town had a Western Union, Jim considered sending a telegram to Austin for delivery to his wife, care of Dr. Vender. If Julia had regained consciousness, the wire would let her know Jim was all right and thinking about her. But he rejected the idea, realizing the message would also provide his present location. He had no intention of making Captain Trumbull's hunt for him any easier. Once he had taken care of Justin Cox, it would be time enough to face the wrath of his commanding officer.

Three days steady riding after leaving Cameron found them approaching Leon County. They had stopped alongside the banks of the Navasota River, the boundary between Robertson and Leon Counties, to let their tired horses drink and graze. While Sizzle and Soot cropped the thick grass next to the stream, their riders sat in the shade and relaxed. Smoky had as usual rolled himself a cigarette. He took a deep pull on the smoke.

"You got any particular ideas in mind about how to go after this Cox character?" he asked Jim.

"Not yet," Jim answered, "although I'm workin' on a couple. But first I want to ride into Centerville. That's where Jim Huggins lives, and with any luck he'll still be home recuperatin'. Since these are his stompin' grounds, I figure he might have some thoughts on what to do."

"That makes sense," Smoky said. "As long as he doesn't know about you defyin' Cap'n Trumbull's orders."

"He probably doesn't. I don't imagine the captain has any idea I headed this far east. And far as we know he still isn't aware you've caught up with me and we're ridin' together. Besides, Jim Huggins and I have been friends a long time. He's saved my life more'n once, and I've done the same for him. I don't think he'd turn me in. But we'll see. If he's not around we'll just have to do our best without him."

"Maybe you should hope Huggins isn't around if he's found out what you did to his son, knockin' the kid unconscious," Smoky said.

"I'll worry about that when we find him."

"How much longer we gonna stay in this spot?" Smoky stretched.

"Rest of the afternoon. If I'm figurin' right, we're only two hours or so out of Centerville. I doubt anyone around here would recognize us, but I'd rather not take the chance. We'll ride in just after sundown."

"You know where Huggins lives?"

"No, but Centerville's a small town from what he tells me. We'll ask around. Shouldn't be too hard to find out."

"Centerville's the Leon County seat. We could stop at the sheriff's office and ask there," Smoky pointed out.

"We could, but the sheriff might be in Cox's back pocket. I'll want to talk to Jim before meetin' up with the local law."

"That sounds like as good a strategy as any. Now I'm gonna get me some shut-eye. I'd recommend you do the same, pardner."

Smoky pulled off his boots, stretched out on his back and tilted his Stetson over his eyes. Jim did likewise.

Early that evening, with twilight descending, the partners reached the outskirts of Centerville.

"From that smell it seems someone is smokin' a whole heap of meat, Jim," Smoky said. "It sure makes my mouth water. I could use a change from your bacon and beans."

"I didn't notice you complainin' about 'em. But you're right. I'd enjoy a change of diet myself," Jim said. "Let's follow our noses and see where they lead."

He pushed Sizzle into a steady jogtrot.

A few minutes later Jim reined in Sizzle and pointed to a small complex of buildings off to the left. The delicious scent they'd been tracking came from a sturdily built smokehouse. In front of that was a small restaurant and store with a sign reading "Woody's Smokehouse" hanging over the door.

"There's our destination, Smoke," Jim said.

"Race you for who buys supper!" his partner challenged.

Smoky jabbed his spurs into Soot's sides, sending the steeldust leaping ahead at a dead run. However, Sizzle, with Jim's urging, soon overtook Smoky's dark gray. When they reached Woody's, Jim's horse was ahead by half a length.

"Looks like you're payin', pardner. Suddenly I'm even hungrier'n I thought I was." Jim grinned.

"I should've known better'n to challenge you to a horse race, even if you're not forkin' Sam," Smoky complained. "After all these years with you as a ridin' pard, you think I'd have learned by now."

Jim swung out of his saddle, looped Sizzle's reins around the hitch rail, and patted the big gelding's shoulder. "Good job, Siz," he praised the horse. Sizzle nickered, gave his rider the equivalent of a horse "kiss" on the nose, then nuzzled Jim's hip pocket. Jim dug out a peppermint and gave it to the paint. "Thanks, Siz," he said. It looks like Julia was right. You're gonna make some kind of a Ranger horse."

Smoky had also dismounted and tied Soot. "Jim, if you're about done spoilin' that horse, let's see what's on the menu," he said.

"Lead the way," Jim answered.

They stepped into the crowded store and eating house.

"I'm gonna be able to fill my belly just fine in this place, Smoke." Jim grinned and rubbed his stomach.

Woody's Smokehouse had all sorts of food-stuffs, both fresh and packaged, available for purchase. And behind the counters, which ran along two sides of the room, hung all manner of smoked and dried meats, including bacon, ham, fowl, venison and a wide variety of sausages. To complement the meats there were many kinds of cheeses, relishes, and pickles. Loaves of fresh-baked bread, fresh-churned butter, plus jars of homemade jams and preserves were in plentiful supply. For drinks there was everything from milk to coffee to beer.

Jim and Smoky stepped up to the counter, where an attractive young black woman greeted them.

"Howdy, gents. My name's Natoshia. Welcome to Woody's. What can I get for you?"

"I'd like a nice thick ham sandwich, no, make that three of 'em, since my pardner's buyin'," Jim requested. "Also a slab of those ribs. A hunk of hard yellow cheese, two pickles, and three sarsaparillas. And I see you've got buttermilk pie. I'll have one of those."

"Do you mean a slice of pie?" Natoshia asked.

"No, I mean an entire pie, oh, and a fork," Jim answered.

Natoshia turned to Smoky.

"How about you, sir?"

"I'll take a slab of ribs, one of those ring sausages, two chunks of hard yellow cheese, and a cold beer," said Smoky. "And half of a cherry pie."

"Certainly. That will be one dollar and seventy five cents, please."

Smoky dug in his pocket and came up with two silver dollars to pay the bill. "Keep the change," he told the waitress.

"Thank you, sir," she replied.

The hungry Rangers worked their way to a corner table, receiving a few curious looks from the other patrons. They dug into their food, eating mostly in silence, enjoying what for hard-riding lawmen used to bacon, beans, and hardtack was a bountiful repast.

Smoky leaned back in his chair, smoking and working on his second beer while Jim finished up his buttermilk pie. Natoshia approached their table, carrying a full pot of coffee and two cups.

"I thought you might like some coffee," she said.

"That's real thoughtful of you, honey," Smoky

answered. "We would enjoy some. Thank you."

"You're welcome." The waitress set the cups on the table and filled them to the brim.

"How was your meal?"

"Everything was real tasty," Jim responded.

"Is there anything else I can get for you?"

"No more food, thanks. We're both ready to bust," Jim said, "but perhaps there is one thing you can tell us. What was your name again?"

"Natoshia. Natoshia Hall. And I'll help if I can."

"Natoshia, we're looking for Jim Huggins. Can you tell us where he lives, and if he's in town?"

"Sergeant Huggins, the Ranger?"

"That's right. We're friends of his."

Jim slipped his hand into his shirt pocket, extracted his badge, and held it in the palm of his hand so only Natoshia could see the silver star on silver circle. He then slid the badge back inside his pocket. "We don't want anyone else to know there are more Rangers in town to meet up with Sergeant Huggins," Jim whispered.

"I understand," Natoshia answered. "His place is just down this road a short way. Turn left from here onto St. Mary's Street, and it's no more than a quarter mile to his home. It's on the right, a yellow brick house. And yes, he is in town. He ate breakfast here this morning."

"We appreciate your help. Thank you."

"You're welcome. And don't worry. No one will find out from me who you gentlemen are."

"Again, thank you," Jim repeated. "And we'll try and stop by again before we leave town. Pay the lady, Smoke."

"I already did."

"For the grub, not the information. Now pay her."

"I reckon I'd better."

Smoky handed two silver dollars to the waitress.

"Now let's get outta here," Jim ordered.

The Rangers headed to their patiently waiting horses.

"You'll be bedded down real soon, Siz," Jim promised his paint while he tightened the cinches. He swung into the saddle. As usual, Smoky rolled and lit a quirly before mounting Soot.

Less than ten minutes later they reined up in front of Jim Huggins' home. It was just as the waitress had described it, a yellow brick house with a large field in the back, rather prepossessing for a Ranger's home. Dusty, Huggins' chestnut gelding, whinnied a loud greeting to the Rangers' mounts from his corral. The welcoming glow of lamplight spilled from several windows onto the road.

"Natoshia gave it to us straight," Jim said. "Looks like Jim's still awake."

"Then let's say howdy," Smoky answered.

They dismounted, tied their horses, and stepped up to the door. Jim rapped on it.

A moment later the door swung open. Jim Huggins stood there, staring in disbelief. "Jim Blawcyzk. It can't be! And Smoky McCue! What're you two ranahans doin' in this neck of the woods?"

"It's us all right," said Jim grinning. "Are you gonna invite us in or leave us standin' out here all night?"

"Of course not. C'mon in." Huggins turned and called to his wife. "Cora! We've got company. Would you please get some coffee boilin'?"

"No need for that," Jim said. "We already ate at that place up the road, Woody's. Great meal. And we need to care for our horses."

"Of course. But what happened to you?" Huggins asked. "You look like you've been through hell and back, Jim. And you don't look all that much better, Smoky."

"I pretty much have been," Jim admitted. "And I guess it shows."

Jim looked all done in. His face was haggard, covered with thick blonde stubble, and his tow hair hung over his collar. He was also coated with dust and dirt. The only washing he'd had in weeks was that at Therese Marchitto's place. Even his blue eyes seemed dull and lifeless.

Smoky looked almost as worn out. He too wore a thick beard in addition to his pencil-thin moustache. His silver-tipped black hair hung lank under his Stetson.

"Boys, let's get your broncs cared for and yourselves cleaned up a mite," said Huggins. "We can talk after that."

The horses settled, Jim and Smoky performed a rudimentary cleanup in the horse trough. Now they, along with Jim and his slim, attractive wife Cora, sat in the Huggins' comfortable living room, cups of steaming black coffee in their hands.

"Nice place you have here," Jim told Huggins. "Sure different from the adobes or clapboard houses I'm used to. And you're lookin' pretty good for a man who took a bullet in the ribs."

"Thanks," Huggins replied. "I'm pretty much recovered. In fact, I just wired Austin yesterday for orders. And we were real lucky to find this house. We bought it from a banker who fell on hard times during the panic a few years back, and needed cash in a hurry. I never could have afforded it on Ranger's pay otherwise."

"Well, it's real cozy. Your wife must get the credit for that. You certainly didn't pretty it up like this," Jim said laughing.

"Thank you," Cora answered. "It's hard to keep up a home, between my working at the school and Jim being gone most of the time, but I do my best."

"You've done a fine job, especially considerin' you've got this 'ol Ranger underfoot," Jim replied.

215

"Jim, stop stallin'. Tell me what the devil you're doin' clear over here in east Texas," Huggins demanded. "And don't tell me you're takin' a vacation."

"I'm not. You've no doubt heard about the raid on my ranch and attack on my family."

"Of course I have," Huggins replied. "I was wondering when you'd get around to that. I'm also aware you pulled a gun on Jeff Timmons and left him tied up, then attacked Dan and took off, leavin' my boy lyin' there out cold. So I'm sure you've already figured out I know you've disobeyed orders, and that Captain Trumbull wants you hogtied and dumped on his desk. Now, you can't just be on the run, or you sure wouldn't have stopped off here. And Smoke, what're you doin' with him? Word I had is Captain Trumbull ordered you to personally run down Jim and bring him in. Jim, the only reason I didn't pull a gun on you as soon as I saw you is we've been friends and ridin' pards far too long for me not to know there's gotta be a good reason for you pullin' all the stunts you have recently. So tell me."

Jim flushed beet red with embarrassment. "Not to mention you didn't shoot me 'cause you weren't holdin' a gun when you answered the door," he said.

"You're stallin' again."

"You're right. I was kinda hopin' you hadn't heard about Dan. So much for that. And I'm plumb sorry, Jim. Sure wish I hadn't had to do that to him. But I didn't have much choice. Cora, I want to apologize to you also."

Jim hesitated, and then continued.

"Captain Trumbull didn't want me goin' after the renegades who shot my boy and, and violated my wife. I just couldn't take those orders. The only reason Dan got caught in the middle is he walked in on me just as I was gettin' ready to leave. I needed time to get a start and couldn't chance him or Jeff reaching headquarters too soon. So I left 'em at my place, as comfortable as I could make 'em."

"Then what?" Huggins asked.

"I headed out lookin' for those *hombres*, and my stolen horses. Found the horses, and some rustlers who'd bought them from the men I was searchin' for. They told me who'd attacked my place. Reese Macklin and his bunch."

"Macklin. I've heard of him. Real bad one, but nobody's been able to pin anything on him."

"They have now. Smoky and I shot it out with Macklin and his men. Most of 'em are dead. Macklin and two others are in jail over in Cameron."

"So if Macklin's outfit is finished what're you doin' here?"

"Macklin wasn't the boss. He was paid to try'n kill me."

"Which means you're here because whoever

217

hired Macklin was from this area. That's the only reason you'd be this far east. You're not claimin' it's someone from right here in Centerville?"

"Close. Read these." Jim pulled the papers he'd taken from Reese Macklin's desk and handed them to Huggins.

Huggins read them thoroughly, his face darkening with anger. "Justin Cox is behind all this? And he waited all these years?" he asked.

"Seems so," Jim replied.

"Hardly seems possible," Huggins responded. "And why didn't Cox come after me and my family? I was there with you on that Texas Pacific case. So was Smoky."

"That's true. But I was in charge of that investigation. You came in later. And Cox probably figured it would be too dangerous goin' after a Ranger in his own back yard. I'm certain he came after me and not you, Jorge, or Smoky because I'm the man who killed his brother."

"So now you're goin' after Justin Cox."

"I plan to. That's where I need your help, Jim. From what Macklin told me it's gonna be darn nigh impossible to get at him. Any chance you could kinda find an excuse to meet Cox, then arrest him?"

"No chance at all, Jim. He doesn't like me, and now I know why. Plus he's always got several bodyguards around, even at county meetings."

"Macklin told us that too," Smoky added.

"So we're gonna have to face Cox on his own turf, seems like," Jim said frowning.

"That's the only way I can see it right now," Huggins conceded. "It's gonna be a fight, that's for certain."

"Any other help we can get? How about your county sheriff?" Jim asked.

"Mike Price? Sure. He and Cox have been at odds for years. He'll want to be in on this."

"Anyone else?"

"Yeah, Sergeant Frank Malinak. He's ridin' over from Bryan to meet with me about the upcoming Delaney trial. He should be here by tomorrow night at the latest. I don't believe either of you have met him."

"I haven't, but I've heard a lot about him, all good." Jim said.

"You'll like him. Frank's a good Ranger. We'll need him and Mike goin' up against Cox. There's no one else I can think of who'll give us a hand."

"I'd like to set up a meeting with your sheriff before Cox gets wind I'm in town and gunnin' for him," Jim said. "We've gotta move fast."

"Fast, but with care," Huggins cautioned. "Look, I've got an idea. Mike Price is giving a birthday party for his Grandma Mamie tomorrow night. She'll be one hundred and four, and she's still sharp as a tack. There'll be a big crowd. No one around here knows you or Smoky, except maybe Cox, and he won't be there. Besides, you two look so ragged it's most likely even he'd never recognize you. I'll talk to Mike in the morning and tell him what you need. We'll go to the party, and then find a way to slip into the back room for a while and have our meeting. We'll just introduce you as deputies from out of town who've worked with Mike before if anyone asks."

"One hundred and four?" Smoky echoed. "That's pretty amazing."

"It sure is," Huggins agreed, "But how about my idea?"

"It should work," Jim said. "Smoke and I can lay low until then."

"There's no need to do that," said Cora. "You'll stay right here. With Laura married and Daniel off with the Rangers we have two empty bedrooms."

"We can't do that. Not as grubby as we are," Jim protested.

"We have two washtubs, and I can heat plenty of water. There's soap, washcloths, and towels. You can bathe in the kitchen. That's the last I'll hear of it. You'll be staying right here as long as you're in town."

"No use arguin' with her, Jim," Huggins laughed.

"I can see I'll get about as far with your wife as I do with mine." Jim smiled. "All right, we'll stay. And I'm more'n ready to hit the sack."

"That's a good idea for all of us, with such a big day ahead tomorrow," Cora said. "Jim can show you to your rooms while I heat your water. The tubs are outside the back door. Just bring them in and fill them. I'll leave you soap and towels. Once you've finished your baths you can just empty the tubs, leave the towels on the back rail, and turn in for the night."

The good nights were said, Jim and Smoky shown their rooms. They came downstairs to find kettles of hot water ready, as promised.

"Sure is gonna feel good to soak off some of this Texas soil, Smoke," Jim remarked.

"Gotta agree with you there, pard," Smoky answered.

The pair of round Number 10 washtubs didn't provide anywhere near the room of a barbershop or hotel's long zinc tubs. Nonetheless, squeezing into those cramped tubs and scrubbing off the grime of the past days was refreshing. They had finished their baths and were toweling off when Smoky eyed Jim.

"Jim, there's somethin' we need to get settled," he said.

"What's that, Smoke?"

"When we meet up with Cox, are you gonna gun him down like you'd planned on doing to Macklin?"

Jim breathed a deep sigh before he responded.

"No, I'm not. I'd purely enjoy that, but I won't.

The best revenge will be bringin' him to trial and disgracing him in front of all his cronies."

"I'm glad to hear you say that," Smoky replied, "Because if you attempted to kill Cox in cold blood I'd have to try and stop you. Or if you did kill him I'd have to arrest you. And we've been pards for so long I'd plumb hate to do either one."

"You don't have to fret on my account," Jim said. "My only plans for Justin Cox are to see him swingin' from the end of a rope. Now let's finish up here and get some shut-eye. And you can sleep as late as you'd like in the morning."

"All right," Smoky said.

Despite Jim's reassurances, once he was in bed Smoky lay on his back on the soft mattress for quite some time, staring at the ceiling.

"Sure wish I could trust Jim," he thought, "but I can't quite believe him. He's still hurtin' real bad over his wife and boy. Well, reckon all I can do is try and stop trouble before it starts."

Smoky rolled onto his stomach. A short while later sleep finally claimed him, but he tossed restlessly all night, unable to erase the cold, dead look in Jim's eyes from his mind.

Chapter 19

The next day the two exhausted Rangers slept late, then ate a leisurely breakfast. They were caring for their horses when Jim Huggins returned from town. Riding alongside him, mounted on a sturdy black and white pinto gelding, was another Ranger. The two men dismounted. Huggins opened the gate and they led their horses into the corral.

"Jim, Smoky, I'd like you to meet Sergeant Frank Malinak. He got into town a mite earlier than planned. Frank, Lieutenant Jim Blawcyzk and Corporal Smoky McCue."

Malinak was the epitome of a Texas Ranger, tall and burly, with dark hair and eyes. He took Jim's hand in a strong grip.

"I'm glad to finally meet you, Lieutenant. Jim's told me some real stories about you."

"And none of them good. I'd bet my hat on that," Jim said laughing. "And the name's Jim. Forget that lieutenant stuff."

"And I'm Smoky," McCue stated, as he shook Malinak's hand.

Huggins and Malinak removed their horses' bridles and saddles. They rubbed them down and turned them loose, then forked hay to them. Afterwards they headed for the trough and splashed cool water over their faces.

Huggins scrutinized Sizzle carefully while Jim finished currying the paint. "Boy howdy, that new horse of yours certainly is a good lookin' animal, Jim," he said.

"Thanks," Jim said. "I'm still gettin' used to ridin' Siz rather'n Sam, but I think he's gonna work out just fine."

"Jim," said Frank Malinak, "Sgt. Huggins told me about what happened to your family. That's a real shame, and there's no punishment harsh enough for the men who did that to your wife and boy. He also told me about what they did to your infamous Sam horse. I was sure sorry to hear about that. I hope I can at least help you bring in the men responsible."

"I appreciate that, Frank," Jim replied.

Jim gave Sizzle a final swipe of the brush, slipped him a peppermint, let the horse nuzzle his shoulder, then ambled over to the fence. "What about tonight? Any news?" he asked Huggins.

"Let's wait until Smoky finishes up," Huggins replied.

"I'm all done," Smoky called as he walked over. He lit the quirly already dangling from his lips.

"We're all set. Mike Price is more'n willin' to cooperate. Far as anyone else is concerned, you two are deputies from Deaf Smith County. You gave me a hand in the past. Since you were passing through town on your way to Houston you stopped over to look me up. You'll ride in separate from me and Frank to help keep folks from suspicionin' we're working together. We'll mingle for a while, and then slip off to meet and formulate our plans. With most of the county there, no one should notice if we're missin' for a while. Most likely they'll figure we've snuck outside to have a pull from the jug, which we will, of course."

"And you're positive neither Cox nor any of his men will be there?" Jim asked. "A politician usually can't resist an event like that. It might look bad if he doesn't make an appearance."

"I'm certain, Jim. There's been bad blood between Price and Cox for years. And Mamie knows Cox for exactly what he is. She gave him what-for at a church social some years back. He's avoided her like the plague ever since."

"Okay, it seems like you've got things well in hand," Jim said. "So where is this party?"

"It's at La Chata, a little Mexican restaurant in the center of town, just down and across the street from the county sheriff's office and jail. You can't possibly miss it. The building's painted a bright kinda orangey-pink color. You'll be surprised at the chuck they serve. It's not the usual *frijoles* like you'd expect in a Mex place. The party starts at seven, so I reckon Cora, Frank, and I will get there about twenty after.

You two *hombres* can wander in shortly after that."

"We're still a mite shaggy-lookin' to attend a fancy party," Smoky said.

"Don't worry about that. This isn't anything real extravagant. Just plenty of good food, drink, and a gathering of Mamie's friends. She's a great gal. Everybody loves her, and she sure won't mind how you look. Besides, even Cora says you chaps cleaned up right nice. Too bad those baths didn't improve your looks any."

"We're too far gone for a plain bath to fix," Jim said smiling. "Since everything's settled, it looks like there's nothing to do until tonight."

"We're as ready as we can be for now. Oh, one more thing before I forget. When you're ridin' by the town square, whatever you do don't try'n shake any nuts off the pecan trees, no matter how tempted you might be to sample a few," Huggins said with a grave look on his face. "Stealin' those pecans will land you in a jail cell real quick. Not even your Ranger badges, Captain Trumbull, or for that matter the governor himself could help you then. We're real protective of our nuts here in Leon County."

"Just the ones on the trees, Jim?" Smoky laughed.

"You can take that any way you'd like, McCue. Meanwhile, Cora should have dinner just about ready. Let's head inside. You can fill Frank in on everything after we eat."

The evening proved to be sultry, with the threat of a thunderstorm hanging in the heavy air. Jim and Smoky took a circuitous route from the Huggins' home to the center of town.

"There's the place," Jim said, indicating a small brightly colored building with "La Chata Mexican Restaurant" painted in brilliant blue, green, and red letters on the sign over the door.

There were so many carriages, buckboards, and horses surrounding the restaurant they were forced to tie their mounts to a hitch rail two blocks away. They looped the reins over the rail, and loosened their cinches.

Sizzle dropped his nose to Jim's hip pocket. Jim gave him a handful of candies. Patting the gelding on the neck, Jim said, "C'mon Smoke, let's head inside and see what's for supper."

The small restaurant was packed, with barely enough space for the Rangers to squeeze through the crowd. Brightly colored paper flowers and streamers decorated the room. In one corner several children were attempting to break open a wildly swinging *piñata.* The deliciously heady odors of highly spiced foods permeated the atmosphere. Just about everyone had plates stacked high with food, while a mariachi band was playing a lively tune. As Huggins had promised, most of the residents of Leon

County had shown up for the affair. Jim asked one attendee where he might find Ranger Jim Huggins. The man waved him toward the back of the room.

Huggins spied Smoky and Jim as they worked their way in his direction.

"Jake Barton!" he called out. "And Frost McDonagh. What the devil brings you two *hombres* to Centerville?"

"There you are, Sergeant," Jim shouted back. "We're headed down to Houston. Gonna do some sightseein'. Since we were passin' through we figured we'd look you up. Man at the general store said we'd find you here. Also said to let folks know he was closing up and would be along shortly himself."

"We kinda worried about hornin' in, but he said we'd be welcome, since this was gonna be the biggest party around here in a month of Sundays," Smoky added.

"That'd be Mort Klein. Well, I'm sure glad he sent you along. And he was right. You are welcome. I'd like you to meet my wife, Cora. Cora, these two *hombres* helped me round up Tom Kane and his bunch up in Deaf Smith County a couple of years back."

Jim lifted his Stetson in greeting. "I'm pleased to meet you, Mrs. Huggins."

"Same here," Smoky added, touching two fingers to the brim of his hat.

"My pleasure, and please, it's Cora." She responded without a hint the two men had spent the previous night in her home.

"And this here's Ranger Frank Malinak," Huggins said.

The three Rangers exchanged handshakes without a sign of ever having met before.

"Now let me introduce you to the guest of honor and her family," Huggins said. He led them to the far side of the restaurant, where several people were in line waiting to express their wishes to Mamie Price.

Huggins called to a lantern-jawed, barrel-chested individual. "Mike! Come over here a minute. Figure I might as well introduce you two to our sheriff while you're waitin'. This party's for his grandmother. She's one hundred and four."

"Mike, I'd like you to meet two real fine lawmen," Huggins said when the sheriff reached them. "These are deputies Jake Barton and Frost McDonagh from Deaf Smith County. Jake, Frost, Sheriff Mike Price."

Price was taller even than the six-foot plus Blawcyzk—and brawny. He shook the Rangers' hands with a bone-crushing grasp. "Anyone who's a friend of Jim is a friend of mine," he boomed. "You gents had anything to drink yet. How about grub?"

"We just got here. Haven't had a chance to get

drinks yet. We wanted to find Jim Huggins first," Jim said. "And meet your grandmother, naturally. It wouldn't be proper to do otherwise."

"Of course," Price replied. "I'll introduce you to her. My family's with her, so you can meet the entire Price clan at the same time. C'mon."

The Leon County sheriff led them to a long, gaily decorated table at the front of the room. Seated at the center was a diminutive elderly woman. Despite her advanced age, her eyes were bright and sparkled with life. A broad smile creased her face while she swayed to the mariachi rhythm.

"Everyone, these are a couple of Jim Huggins' friends, deputies Jake Barton and Frost McDonaugh from Deaf Smith County way. Jake, Frost, this lovely lady is my wife, Joetta. Alongside her is our oldest daughter, Amanda Payne. Next to her are her sisters Stephanie and Pam. Amanda's kids, my grandson Price and granddaughter Calee are around here somewhere. They're probably tryin' to bust open that *piñata*. And then we have my sister Linda. And lastly, but hardly least the two ladies in the middle are my mother Noveline and grandmother Miss Mamie. And don't worry. I sure don't expect you to remember all their names."

"We appreciate that." Jim laughed.

"I'd sure like a birthday kiss from you two handsome fellas," Mamie requested. "The tow-headed one with those nice blue eyes first."

"Of course, Miss Mamie," Jim said. He leaned down to kiss her on the cheek. When he did, Mamie whispered to him.

"You're no deputy. Neither is your partner. You're both Texas Rangers."

"How'd you know that? Did Mike tell you?" Jim whispered.

"No. But I can tell you're Rangers. You have the look about you, just like Jim Huggins. Don't worry. I realize you must have a good reason for keeping your identity confidential. Your secret is safe with me."

"Thank you, ma'am," Jim replied. He kissed her once again.

Smoky also took his turn kissing the guest of honor. Mamie hugged him so tightly it took his breath away. "Ma'am, if I weren't already married, I'd propose to you right now," he said once he was released.

"Who said I'd have you?" Mamie said.

"I guess she told you . . . Frost." Jim nearly slipped and called Smoky by his rightful name.

"Well, now that you've met the family, why don't you boys circulate for a while," Mike suggested. "Get some food and drinks too. The *quesadillas* here are especially good, and the tequila will knock your boots off."

The two Rangers headed for the serving tables, which held an astounding variety and quantity of

Mexican and Texan dishes. They soon had plates piled high, Smoky a glass of fiery tequila, Jim a bottle of sarsaparilla. Frank Malinak joined them.

"Jim wasn't kiddin'," Smoky remarked to him. "Most of the county must've turned out."

"Just about," Malinak said munching a *jalapeño* pepper. "There are even a couple of reporters from two of the outlying towns here, besides the one from the *Centerville News*. See that man and woman talkin' in the corner? The woman's Kristy Vandegriff, who reports for the *Jewett Messenger*. The man with her is Hank Hargrave, owner and publisher of the *Normangee Star*. I reckon this affair's gonna be the social event of the year in Leon County. C'mon, I'll introduce you to a few more folks I happen to know."

Frank brought them to a group standing near the front door.

"Folks, I'd like you to meet a couple of men who helped Jim Huggins up in the Panhandle a few years back, deputies Frost McDonagh and Jake Barton. Frost, Jake, say howdy to Ken Jones and his wife Martha. Then we have Becky Hines, and finally Dawson and Doreen Jordan of the Double DJ Ranch. Their spread's one of the biggest in these parts. Now I've got to head back and talk with Jim for a bit, so I'll leave all of you to get acquainted."

Jim and Smoky spent a few minutes conversing with the Leon County folks, until from the corner of his eye Jim saw Mike Price nod to him. Jim nodded in return and made his excuses to leave. He edged his way through the crowd and outside. Making sure he was unobserved, he ducked around the back of the restaurant. Smoky soon followed.

The only illumination in the small lot behind the restaurant was provided by the setting quarter moon and the lightning bugs flickering in the bushes.

Jim declined the clay jug Mike Price offered. Smoky accepted. Taking a long pull of the contents, he gasped as the fiery liquor hit his throat.

"What's in this stuff?" he said nearly choking.

"That's our secret family recipe," Mike said chuckling.

"Well, it dang near killed me." Smoky pulled out the makings and began rolling a cigarette.

"Enough. We'd best start talkin' before we're missed," Jim said.

"In another minute. We're waiting on one more," Huggins answered.

"I'm right here." Dawson Jordan stepped into the clearing.

"What's he doin' here?" Jim demanded. "Last thing we need is word gettin' out about what we're up to."

"Take it easy, Lieutenant," Huggins answered. "I asked Dawson to join us. We need his help if we're to have any prospect at all of gettin' to Justin Cox."

"Dawson, you've probably already guessed, but these men aren't deputy sheriffs. This is Texas Ranger Lieutenant Jim Blawcyzk and his pardner, Corporal Smoky McCue. We don't have time to explain everything right now, but they're in town to arrest Justin Cox."

"It's about time," Jordan responded. "Cox's been ridin' roughshod over folks for far too long, hidin' behind his political connections. He would've been taken down long ago if it weren't for his friends in Austin. You'll get whatever you need from me."

"We're gonna need your place to reach Cox, hopefully before he realizes what's happening," Huggins answered.

"Dawson and Doreen's Double DJ abuts Cox's Circle Bar C," said Mike Price. "Cox has been hassling the Jordans for years, trying to get their land. So far they've been able to hold him off, but he's got a lawsuit pending in Austin right now, and with his influence up there he's likely to win. And if he doesn't he'll try another way. Jim, you've seen firsthand what Cox will do when he's thwarted. He's ambitious, ruthless, and vindictive."

"That still doesn't explain why we need Dawson's help," Jim said.

"The Double DJ sits on a rise overlooking

the Circle Bar C, Jim. We can check over the situation before we ride in. There's a creek which marks the boundary between the two places. Plenty of scrub grows along the banks, so we'll have some good cover."

"I'd still like to try by myself, or maybe me and Smoke, ridin' in, grabbin' Cox, and ridin' back out again, without any shootin'," Jim said.

"You're sure you don't mean ridin' in, plugging Cox, then ridin' away, Jim?" Smoky challenged.

"No, I don't. Much as I'd like to put a couple of bullets in his lousy guts, I've already told you I want him brought to trial."

"Stop it, both of you," Huggins said stepping between the two Rangers. "Arguin' amongst ourselves won't get us anywhere. As far as one or two men ridin' into Cox's place, that's a real bad idea at best, suicidal at worst. You might reach Cox, but you'd never get out again. You'd be shot to ribbons. You asked for my help, Lieutenant, and I'm givin' it to you straight. The only chance we have of arresting Justin Cox is the five of us."

"The six of us," Jordan spoke up. "You're not leaving me out of the fun."

"Okay," said Huggins, "the six of us goin' in there ready for a gunfight. To borrow your favorite phrase, Jim, you can bet a hat on it, there will be gunplay."

"All right. We're gonna have to shoot it out

with Cox's men," Jim said. "How many will we be up against?"

"He's got about twenty or so ridin' for him," Huggins answered. "Some of 'em are ordinary cowpokes, so those *hombres* might not put up much of a fight. But Cox has got eight or nine gunslingers workin' for him. The worst one's probably Mike Buckley."

"Macklin mentioned him," said Smoky.

"I've never run across him, but I understand he's lightning fast and a dead aim with a six-gun, as well as poison mean," Malinak added. "There are no warrants out on him in Texas, but he's supposed to have killed several men over in New Mexico territory, and there are also warrants out for him in Nebraska and Missouri. He's the one who'll give us the most trouble."

"Any kids or women we have to worry about?" Jim asked.

"I don't believe so," Price answered. "Cox's wife left him and moved back to Iowa years ago. She took the kids with her. They'd be grown up by now. Only female on the place will be his Mexican cook and housekeeper. She's an old woman, so I'm sure once the shootin' starts she'll hole up."

"That settles things," said Jim rubbing his jaw. "We'll meet at the Double DJ, and then ride on the Circle Bar C. "How far is it to your place, Dawson?"

"It's about six miles south of here."

"You're not planning on headin' down there right now, are you?" Price asked. "It'd be hard to explain why I'm leavin' my own grandma's birthday party."

"Not right now. We'd give ourselves away," Jim replied. "We'll head back inside and do some more celebratin'. But I intend to strike Cox's place at sunup. Any objections?"

"Just one," said Smoky. "Dawson, what about your wife? How will she feel about this? After all, if things go wrong you could lose your ranch."

"Or your life," Malinak added.

"Doreen will be with us one hundred percent," Jordan answered. "She's as tired of Cox's antics as I am. If someone doesn't put a stop to his ruthless shenanigans we'll lose our place in any event. Better to go down fightin' than to just roll over and play dead."

"Any other questions?" Jim asked.

He was met with silence and the shaking of heads.

"Then let's head back to the party. We'll ride separately to the Double DJ. Figure on arrivin' there so everyone gets a couple hours sleep. But we'll be ridin' at dawn."

Chapter 20

The next morning, despite the early hour, Doreen Jordan insisted on cooking breakfast for the lawmen before they rode against the Circle Bar C. The Rangers, sheriff, and their hosts ate silently in the pre-dawn darkness, each one thinking of the chore ahead.

"Would you like some more coffee, Jim?" Doreen asked Blawcyzk.

"Another cup," he answered. "And Doreen, I've got to be absolutely certain so I'm gonna ask you once more. Are you sure it's all right our usin' your home like this?"

"I'm positive," she said. "And I also agree with Dawson's decision to ride with you. The survival of our ranch is at stake."

"Then all I can say is I'm grateful to the both of you. We all are."

Once they had finished eating, the men headed for the corrals. It was shortly before dawn by the time their horses were saddled.

Jim slipped Sizzle a peppermint, then swung onto the tall gelding's back. "You boys ready to ride?"

"Let's give Dawson a minute with his wife," Smoky suggested.

"All right. We'll take five minutes." Jim conceded.

The others waited in their saddles, Smoky as always working on a quirly, while Jordan and Doreen made their farewells. Finally, the rancher kissed his wife and climbed onto his wide-backed bay.

"I'm ready," he said.

"Then let's go." Jim dug his heels into Sizzle's flanks, sending the paint forward at a jogtrot. The others strung out behind him headed for the creek which marked the boundary between the Double DJ and the Circle Bar C. It was a thirty minute ride from the Dawson's ranch house.

Blawcyzk reined to a halt at the summit of the hill overlooking the Circle Bar C. He waved Jordan up alongside him. "All right Dawson, this is your home stompin' grounds. You still think we don't have a chance of gettin' onto the Circle Bar C without bein' spotted?"

"There's a chance, but it's highly unlikely," Jordan answered. "Cox always has riders out patrolling the perimeters of his spread. And if we get past them he's got Mike Buckley and a few more like him waitin'. So unless I miss my guess we're in for a real shootin' scrape."

"Where would you choose if you had to pick a spot to try'n sneak up on 'em?" Jim asked.

"See that bend in the creek. You can't see much of the bank on the other side because the brush is so thick, but it's pretty steep there, so it'll keep us out of sight until we top it. That thick scrub'll help hide us too."

"Then that's what we'll do." Jim pulled out his field glasses to study the Circle Bar C. "Reese Macklin wasn't lyin'," he said. "That place is gonna be tough."

The Circle Bar C's buildings sat on a high ridge, with cleared pastures and corrals extending in all directions. There was virtually no cover once past the creek. The main house and bunkhouse were solid brick and adobe, with small windows that would make it difficult to hit a target inside. Once the lawmen started up that hill they would be clear marks for any defenders.

"We might have one advantage, surprise," Malinak said. "They sure won't be expectin' us."

"It doesn't look as if anyone's stirrin' yet either," Price added. "Maybe we can get in close before they realize what's happening."

"You want to go in there on foot or horseback, Jim?" Huggins asked.

"Horseback, at least until we get in close. We'd be smaller targets on foot, but I'd rather have the horses handy in case we need them. We'll ride to just below the top of that ridge, then dismount and lead the broncs. And we're still gonna try and get Cox to give himself up without a fight."

"Glad to hear you've changed your mind about killin' him," Smoky said.

"Yeah. But if I think about Julia too long I might just reconsider," Jim answered.

"Cox'll never surrender, especially knowing he's lookin' at a long prison term, or the gallows," Malinak predicted.

"Well, whatever we're gonna do we'd best do it right quick. Sittin' around here jawin' all morning ain't gettin' anything done," McCue said. He still harbored a suspicion Jim would gun Cox down the minute he got him in his sights.

"You're right, Smoke," Jim agreed. "Check your guns, then we'll head on in."

He pinned his hand carved silver star on silver circle badge to his vest. Smoky, Jim Huggins, and Frank did likewise.

The riders eased their horses down the incline to the creek bed.

"That brush is gonna make a lot of noise when we push through it, Jim," Smoky observed.

"It can't be helped. We'll just have to be ready for anyone who hears us comin'," said Jim. He heeled Sizzle into a walk. The big paint snorted a mild protest when Jim forced him into the scrub lining the stream bank. The other horses and riders followed close behind as Jim's horse bulldozed a path through the thick bushes and tangled vines.

Despite the thorny brambles clawing his hide and the whipping branches stinging his flanks, Sizzle plunged across the creek and up the opposite bank. Jim reined him to a stop halfway up the incline. Mike Price pulled his dun up alongside them.

"If I ever need someone to plow through a thicket I'm gonna borrow your cayuse, Jim," the sheriff said. "He sure made it easy for the rest of us."

"That's probably as easy as things are gonna get," Malinak said.

"Let's find out. Dismount. We're walkin' from here." Jim swung out of his saddle. The others followed suit.

Guns at the ready, leading their horses, they swiftly climbed toward the top of the ridge.

"So far, so good," Smoky commented when they reached the summit unchallenged. "No one's spotted us."

"Except for that rider over there."

Jordan indicated a horseman approaching at a fast trot, his Winchester out and leveled. When six-guns were aimed at his chest, the rider jerked his mount to a halt, tossed the rifle aside, and raised his hands over his head.

"Get off your horse. No fast moves or we'll blast you to Kingdom Come," Jim ordered.

The rider dismounted and stood alongside his horse, hands still raised. "What's goin' on here? Who are you?" he demanded.

"Texas Rangers. We're lookin' for your boss, Justin Cox. Cooperate with us and you won't have any trouble. Don't and you'll be headed for prison," Jim answered. "What's your name?"

"Zack. Zack King."

"Well, Zack King, is Cox at home?"

"He sure is," the shaken King answered. "But you'll never get to him. He's been on the prod for quite some time now. He's taken on half a dozen more gunmen over the past several weeks."

"You happen to know why?"

"Just rumors is all," King shrugged. "Word is he's afraid the Rangers are after him. I dunno why. But it looks like he was right."

"You got names for any of those new gunmen?"

"Yeah. Haney Scott's one of 'em. Bud Sliney's another."

"Two of the most vicious killers in Texas," Huggins said.

"Yeah, but neither of 'em's as ornery as Mike Buckley. He's one mean cuss, and still Cox's head honcho," King answered.

"Frank, tie our friend up," said Jim, "Gag him too. We'll pick him up later."

Malinak took a length of rope from his saddle-bag and bound King tightly, hand and foot. He took King's own bandanna, knotted it, and shoved it in his mouth as a gag. "I wouldn't try too hard to pull that gag out, fella. You might choke yourself to death," he advised.

"Let's move," Jim ordered. "And stay alert. We

can be sure there's more outriders watching for intruders."

His words proved prophetic. A moment later another rider appeared at the top of the ridge. Unlike King, this man immediately pulled out his pistol and fired a quick shot, which just missed Mike Price's throat. The sheriff jerked sideways when the slug burned a streak along the side of his neck. The lawmen returned fire, their bullets rolling the gunman out of his saddle with his chest full of lead.

"They'll have heard those shots. There's no chance of doin' this without a fight now. Mount up!" Jim shouted.

The six men swung into their saddles. Jim urged Sizzle into a dead run, the other horses strung out behind. They topped the hill to see men spilling from the bunkhouse. More were emerging from the main house, while still more riders galloped in their direction. Not expecting trouble, most didn't have guns at the ready. Several were hastily buckling gunbelts around their waists.

"Spread out, and keep them covered," Jim shouted.

The lawmen pulled their horses to a halt. They kept their revolvers leveled at the men gathering in the yard, as well as the horsemen.

Two more men emerged from the main house and stood on the porch. One was young, in his early twenties, big and husky and broad through the body, with a good-sized paunch pushing out his gunbelt. He had dark hair and eyes; a thin brown beard framed his jaw. His movements were slow and indolent, but the hand resting on the butt of a heavy Remington .44 on his right hip belied his sluggishness. His general appearance marked him as a dangerous man and a pitiless killer. This was Mike Buckley. The other, Justin Cox, was middle-aged, with thinning salt and pepper hair and dark eyes that glittered malevolently. He glared at the intruders, then his gaze settled on Jim Blawcyzk. His expression turned to one of pure hatred.

"The upstairs windows, Jim," Huggins whispered. He lifted his Winchester from its scabbard to cover them.

Two men with rifles had appeared in those windows.

"I see 'em," Jim whispered back. "Don't see Sliney or Scott anywhere. That's probably them."

He raised his voice. "Don't anybody move, or there'll be a bloodbath here today," he said. "We've got no argument with most of you men."

"What exactly are you doing here, Lieutenant Blawcyzk?" Cox demanded. "I heard you were dead, killed in an attack on your ranch. Later I found out the news of your demise was obviously premature, and you had somehow survived. I must say I was extremely disappointed to hear that. And I am just as surprised to find you invading my home."

Wordlessly, Mike Buckley started to lift the Remington from its holster.

"Don't do anything yet, Mike," Cox ordered. "I want to hear what the lieutenant has to say."

Buckley let the gun slide back in place.

"Well, Lieutenant?" Cox urged.

"You weren't surprised about that attack, since you planned and paid for it." Jim said through clenched teeth. "That's why we're here. To arrest you, Justin Cox, for conspiracy to murder a peace officer, and conspiracy to commit murder, robbery, rape, assault, and horse stealin'. I'm sure we can add a few more charges too. We'll also be checkin' to see how many men on the Ranger Fugitive List might be here."

"That accusation is so patently absurd it would be laughable, but the impugning of my reputation is something I cannot tolerate," Cox responded. "I had nothing to do with the invasion of your home. And I certainly have no idea who was responsible. I also must emphatically state all of my men are merely cowhands. None of them are wanted."

"Hold it, you!" Malinak suddenly shouted. "Less'n you want a slug through your guts!" He thumbed back the hammer of his Colt and aimed it at the belt buckle of a lanky gunman who'd attempted to ease his six-gun from its holster unnoticed.

"Cox, tell your men to keep their hands clear of their guns," Jim reiterated.

"Let the lieutenant finish speaking his piece," Cox said.

"Mike Buckley's standin' next to you. He's a wanted man in several jurisdictions," Jim replied. "Moreover, you hired Reese Macklin and his outfit to kill me and attack my family. And you might've gotten away with it, except Macklin made one big mistake. He didn't make sure I was dead."

"That ridiculous allegation is completely false," Cox retorted. "I have no idea who this Reese Macklin is."

"You sure do," Jim shot back. "He's in jail right now in Cameron, along with a couple of his men. I put him there. He confessed to everything, and implicated you."

"Why would I be involved with such a scheme?"

"To get revenge on me for what happened to your brother."

"That's insane. It's true I despise you for killing Thaddeus, but I would never stoop to cold-blooded murder. And you have no way to prove otherwise. All you have is the word of a common criminal, who no doubt came up with this wild story to save his own neck."

"Macklin kept a record of his dealings with you, Cox. I've got them, and they're the evidence that will send you to prison for a long time, maybe the rest of your life."

Mike Buckley spoke up for the first time. The threat in his otherwise soft-spoken voice was plain. "I think we've wasted enough time palaverin', Ranger. I've killed me a couple of lawmen in New Mexico and Nebraska, but none yet in Texas. I figure it's high time I made up for that oversight. You just say the word, and we'll go for our guns whenever you're ready. It'd give me pure pleasure to sink a couple of slugs in your belly."

The sleepy-eyed killer tensed, his right hand hovering over the butt of his Remington.

Cox put a restraining hand on Buckley's arm. "Not quite yet, Mike," he ordered.

"Lieutenant, all I have to do is give the word for you and your men to be cut to ribbons. And Jordan, I don't have to tell you what will happen to your wife once you're dead. I'll have your spread for pennies on the dollar, and toss her out on the streets. She'll end up making a living as a common trollop. You might want to think about that."

"I've made my choice, Cox. So's Doreen. You're finished in this county," Jordan responded.

"If that's how you want things," Cox shrugged. "I think we've said everything that needs sayin'."

"Not quite," Jim said. Before Cox could protest, he turned to the gathered Circle Bar C men. "Your boss here arranged to have me killed. Now, that might not bother many of you all that much. But the men he hired attacked and brutally violated my wife. They also shot down my son. That's the kind of man you're working for, a man who would have an innocent woman beaten and raped and a thirteen year-old boy gunned down. You all think about that, and if that's the kind of man you want to die for."

"I've heard enough," Cox screamed. He snaked a hand inside his coat and pulled out a short-barreled revolver. He fired one quick shot, then dove back inside the door. His hastily fired bullet missed Blawcyzk by two feet. Mike Buckley also jerked his gun and fired. His slug took the hat from Smoky McCue's head. McCue's return shot missed as Buckley followed Cox through the door. Sizzle whinnied in pain when a bullet scored his flank, but stood steady under Jim's firm hand.

Instantly, the grounds of the Circle Bar C erupted in gunfire. Jim and his men dove from their saddles, shooting as they scattered for cover. A number of Cox's men went down at the first volley. Others raised their hands and raced for cover, wanting no part of this fight. Evidently Blawcyzk's speech had had its effect, at least on some of the Circle Bar C hands.

Jim Huggins had blasted the second floor window panes to bits, his rifle fire driving the men behind them back so quickly they hadn't been able to get off a shot. Now he took up a position at the corner of the house, blazing away. One gunman's bullet drove splinters of wood from a board just over Huggins' head. Huggins return shot tore through the man's right shirt pocket and into his lung, spinning him to the dirt.

Mike Price, Frank Malinak, and Smoky McCue had taken shelter behind a woodpile, from where they had a good field of view of the bunkhouse. Several of the Circle Bar C gunmen had retreated there. Others had withdrawn to the protection of the barn. All these were exchanging a heated fire with the three lawmen.

Dawson Jordan was huddled behind a rain barrel. Bullets punctured the barrel, sending spurts of water over the rancher as they sought him out. One gunman attempted to rush the Double DJ owner, only to die when Jordan put a bullet through his chest. Jordan settled back to outwait the siege, his carefully timed bullets taking some of the pressure off the lawmen.

Jim Blawcyzk rolled down the yard's slight slope and bellied down behind an ornamental shrub. One of Cox's men managed to circle behind the Ranger and draw a bead on Jim's broad back. Just before he pulled his trigger, Malinak spotted him, whirled, and snapped off a shot. The gunman screeched in agony as Malinak's bullet buried itself in his stomach. He clamped a hand to his middle, staggering. Malinak put a finishing slug into his chest.

Jim spun at the gunman's scream, saw him go down at the second hit, and waved his gratitude to the sergeant. He emptied the spent cartridges from his Peacemaker and reloaded.

Mike Buckley climbed, unseen, onto the roof of the main house. He aimed at Blawcyzk, thumbed back the hammer of his Remington, and pulled the trigger. His bullet took Jim in the right side just below his ribs. Jim was knocked back by the shock of the slug's impact.

Buckley once more took deliberate aim at Jim's chest. Before he could fire again, the Ranger put two bullets into his belly, then slammed three more into the center of his chest. The brawny gunman crumpled, and rolled down the roof and over the edge. He crashed onto a ramshackle outhouse, his bulk collapsing the dilapidated structure. Buckley's body lay motionless amidst the shattered boards and muck.

Two men climbed to the barn's hayloft where they had a better angle to blast Price, McCue, and Malinak from cover. One's bullet punctured Price's left arm. The sheriff's return shot ripped through the gunman's stomach. He screamed, dropped his rifle, half-rose, then doubled over and plunged from the loft, thudding in the dirt below.

Smoky aimed at the other gunman's beltline and fired. His bullet caught the outlaw just above the belt buckle, plowing deep into his guts. The man clawed desperately at his bullet-torn belly, staggered, and fell alongside his partner.

Several men burst from the back of the house spraying a wall of fire to keep Blawcyzk's men pinned down. Cox crouched in their midst as they dashed for the barn. Forced into cover by the hail of lead, the lawmen were unable to stop them. The renegades made the stable. Three of them stopped at the door and kept up a steady fire while the rest disappeared inside. Moments later, Cox and the others burst from the stable, spurring their horses into a dead run.

Two of the three men who'd covered Cox's escape also made their horses and galloped after the others. The third died when Smoky put a bullet into his back. He fell on his face in the stable doorway.

Seeing Cox escaping, and many of their number dead or wounded, the remainder of the Circle Bar C men decided they wanted no more of the fight. A white rag tied to a rifle barrel was poked from the bunkhouse door.

"We've had enough. We're surrenderin'," a shaky voice called.

"Toss out your guns and come out with your hands in the air," Jim ordered.

He hurried up to where his men waited, covering the ranch hands while they emerged from the bunkhouse. "You boys all right?" he asked.

In addition to Price's punctured arm, Jordan had blood from a bullet graze trickling down his left cheek.

"We're fine," Price answered.

"Price, I'm leavin' you and Dawson in charge of these prisoners. We can sort everything out later. Rest of us are goin' after Cox."

"Wait a minute. What about you, Jim?" McCue questioned, looking at the blood-soaked side of Blawcyzk's shirt. "Appears like you're bleedin' pretty heavy."

"I'm all right."

Blawcyzk pulled the bandanna from his neck and stuffed it inside his shirt in an effort to staunch the flow of blood.

"I'll get our horses."

Blawcyzk whistled, and Sizzle trotted up to him, nuzzling his face.

"How bad you hurt, bud?" Jim asked. He ran a gentle hand over the bullet wound on the paint's flank, finding to his relief it was merely a shallow gash. Already the blood coating it was half dried. "You'll be all right, Siz. I'll get to that cut soon as I can."

Jim swung into the saddle and rounded up the Rangers' scattered horses. Sizzle herded them back to their waiting riders. The men grabbed the horses' trailing reins and leapt onto their backs.

"Those renegades headed north," said Huggins. "Looks like they're aimin' for old Fort Boggy. We'll have a devil of a time roustin' 'em out of there if they make it."

"What's Fort Boggy?" Blawcyzk asked.

"The site of an early Ranger encampment, back in the forties," Huggins explained. "Indians also used the spot for a campground. It's kind of hilly, especially for this part of Texas, and there's also a lot of bottomlands and swamp. Plenty of places for those renegades to hole up and ambush us. Lots of game in there, some of it almost as ornery as the men we're chasin'. Gators and javelinas, and plenty of cottonmouths too. Probably the worst are the wild boars. You sure don't want to face one of them if he's riled. Which they are all of the time."

"How far to there?" Jim asked.

"Six miles, more or less," Huggins answered. "I figure those boys have a mile or two head start on us. It's gonna be close."

"We'll make it," Jim shot back. He dug bootheels into Sizzle's flanks, sending the big paint leaping forward. The others followed close behind.

Shortly, Huggins called a halt. Their horses

stood, blowing. "That's old Fort Boggy just ahead, Jim," he said. "Their tracks lead right in there. Hoofprints of ten horses, I'd say, so that means we're facin' ten men, probably includin' Sliney and Scott. They could be hidin' in any of a hundred or more spots."

"They might've split up, too," Malinak added.

"How do you want to handle it, Lieutenant?" McCue asked.

"You know the place better'n any of us, Jim. How would you manage it?" Jim asked Huggins.

"They won't be able to hide their trail. Too much soft ground and mud," Huggins answered. "I'd say we should just follow the prints. If they split up then we can split up. But we'll have to be mighty careful. The brush is so thick in places a man could be two feet from you and you'd never see him. Only way you'd find out he's there was when his bullet hit you."

"Sure wish Sam was under me," Jim said sighing. "He'd smell out any of 'em holed up like that. I'm not sure Siz will. Well, let's get after those *hombres*. Like Jim said, slow and careful. Once we get an idea where they might be at we'll go in on foot. Jim, you take the lead."

Huggins urged his chestnut gelding Dusty to the head of the column. Single file, the men headed into the nearly impenetrable maze of swamps, bottomlands, and thickets that marked old Fort Boggy.

Twenty minutes later, Huggins raised his hand. "We'd better dismount," he said. "I've got a pretty good idea where we'll find 'em. There's a good sized hollow about a quarter mile ahead. There's only a couple trails into it. It's got an abandoned settler's dogtrot cabin in the center. When I was a kid, my buddies and I used that shack for a fort while we played at fightin' Comanches or Mexicans. The brush around it is well nigh impossible to penetrate, except for those two trails. And most places you can't see a foot into that scrub. I'd wager those renegades are burrowed down in there, just waitin' for us to ride up so they can blast us from our saddles before we even know what hit us. They've probably realized they can't outrun us, so they've set up a nice little bushwhackin'. In fact, if I were the lieutenant, I'd bet my hat on it. But we're gonna turn the tables."

"How so?" McCue asked.

"I've hunted all through here since I was a kid," Huggins answered. "I know every inch of that hollow, and the thickets surroundin' it. There's a couple of rabbit paths where we can belly through the brush. There's also some big cypress trees along the stream in that hollow we can use for cover. We'll surprise them with a bushwhackin' of our own. But we'll have to go the rest of the way on foot."

"You're still in charge, Jim," Blawcyzk told him.

The horses were tied, Winchesters pulled from saddle scabbards, pockets stuffed with extra shells. Spurs were removed, any other item the men wore or carried that might clink or otherwise make noise discarded.

"Let's go," Huggins ordered.

Before they reached the hollow's perimeter, Huggins led them onto a dim, almost invisible deer track. Five minutes later, at the edge of a tangle of brush and blackberry brambles, he called a halt.

"Okay, here's where we split up," he whispered. "Frank and I'll head left. We'll reach one trail to the hollow in about three minutes. Jim, you and Smoke go right at that dead cottonwood. A bit beyond that you'll see a small opening in the brush, down low. You'll have to get down and crawl on your bellies for a couple hundred feet, but that rabbit path will get you to the hollow."

Huggins hesitated, looking at Jim's blood-soaked side. The lieutenant's breathing was harsh, his face pale. "Jim, can you make it all right?" he asked.

"I'll make it. It's just a flesh wound."

"What's the situation when we get there?" McCue asked.

"I'm figurin' they'll have left a few men in the brush. The others will be holed up in that run-down cabin. They'll be thinking we'll be easy targets, but they'll be in for a surprise when we sneak up on 'em through the brush. It'll be tough, but we'll flush 'em outta there."

"What about the ones in the brush?"

"Hopefully, Smoke, once we open up on the men in the cabin the ones in the thickets will start shootin' back at us, which will give their positions away. Once that happens it'll be a simple matter of us pluggin' them before they plug us."

"Unless they spot us first," Malinak pointed out.

"That's a distinct possibility," Huggins agreed. "Just be real careful, and if you should happen on one of 'em make sure you get him before he can shout out a warning. Any other questions?"

Silence.

"Good, we'll start in now. In ten minutes we should all be in place. Once you hear my first shot just pour it on 'em hot and heavy. We're outnumbered, so I don't have to tell you make every shot count. Time to move."

Huggins and Malinak disappeared into the thick undergrowth. Jim and Smoky found the path Huggins had indicated, then dropped to their stomachs. Pushing their Winchesters ahead of them, they began the laborious crawl toward the hollow.

Arching boughs slapped at the Rangers, stinging their faces, and thorny branches clawed at their clothes and tore their skin. The soft, muddy ground soaked the front of their garments, while the hot, humid air drained their strength. By the time they reached the hollow's edge, they were filthy, bloodied, and drenched with sweat.

"There's the cabin," Jim whispered when the abandoned structure came into view just beyond the scrub.

"Seems like it's occupied, too," Smoky answered. "There's horses tied out back, and I glimpsed some movement in the doorway.

"I'll head east about a hundred feet, Smoke," Jim said. "Then all we have to do is wait for Jim's signal."

He wriggled into the underbrush, soon out of Smoky's sight. Finding a slight gap in the bushes which allowed a good view of the cabin and its surroundings, Jim settled down to wait. He pulled out his Colt and laid it within easy reach, while holding his Winchester at the ready.

The heat was almost unbearable. Flies and mosquitoes tormented Jim, drawn to him by the blood soaking his shirt. Sweat rolled off his forehead and into his eyes. Several times he had to wipe them to clear his vision. When a thud, followed by a low grunt, came from Smoky's direction, Jim jerked up his head in surprise.

"Smoky. Smoke!"

There was no response.

"Smoke!" Jim called once more.

Again, only deafening silence.

Jim started back to find what had happened to his partner when a puff of dust appeared in front of the outlaws' horses, followed by the sharp crack of a rifle echoing across the hollow. Several more shots followed in quick succession, the bullets striking the ground around the horses' hooves. Terrified by the shots and the bullets ricocheting under them, the panicked animals pulled away from their picket line and galloped off.

Shouted curses emanated from the cabin as the outlaws realized they had just lost their means of escape. Their gunshots converged on the spot in the brush where the hidden gunman had opened fire. However, Jim Huggins had already rolled to a different location.

Two of Cox's men dashed from the cabin and chased after the fleeing mounts, only to be cut down by Ranger lead. Haney Scott ran into the dogtrot between the two rooms of the cabin, going to his knees and aiming at where he'd seen a puff of powder smoke from Huggins' Winchester. Jim drew a bead on Scott and fired, his bullet slamming into the gunslinger's chest and driving him backwards. Scott went down hard.

Several gunmen opened up from the brush, firing at the smoke from the Ranger guns. Like the Rangers, these experienced fighters rolled or crawled to a new position every time they fired a shot.

The lawmen concentrated their fire on the cabin, only taking a shot at the men in the brush when fairly confident of making a hit. Malinak fired immediately to the left of where he'd seen a puff of smoke. His bullet found its mark. The hidden gunman screeched in agony, then stumbled out of the brush, doubled over clutching his stomach. He staggered for a few steps, dropped to his hands and knees to crawl several feet, then fell on his face. He twitched once, and lay unmoving.

Jim rolled onto his back at the sudden rustling of brush behind him. A pasty-faced outlaw dove from the bushes, a long-bladed knife in his hand. Jim triggered his Peacemaker, the .45 slug tearing into the man's stomach, ripping through him and coming out his back. He collapsed on top of the Ranger, the blade of his knife tearing Jim's shirt along his short ribs before being driven into the ground. Jim shoved the dying gunman off him.

The fight raged on, the outlaws unable to get a clear shot at the bushed-up Rangers, the lawmen blazing away without much effect at the men in the run-down dogtrot cabin,

Smoky did put a bullet through one gunman's side. The desperado's rifle spilled from his hands. He slumped over the windowsill. Another gunman took his place, firing back at McCue. His bullet clipped Smoky's shoulder, but he was clearly framed in the window as he fired. Jim Huggins shot him in the chest.

"I've gotta try and draw 'em outta there," Jim muttered. He emptied his pockets of rifle shells to reload his Winchester. That done, he rose to his feet and zigzagged across the open ground between the brush and the cabin, firing as rapidly as he could work the lever of his rifle. His partners covered him with an equally rapid fire.

Just when Jim reached the bank of the creek a shot cracked from the brush. He screeched in agony, grabbed his chest, and tumbled down the bank to lay face-down and motionless in the shallow, murky water.

Jim Huggins shouted from the brush.

"Frank! Smoky! They just downed Jim! It's time to end this one way or the other. We're gonna charge those sons of Satan. Now!"

Huggins jumped from his cover, McCue and Malinak doing likewise. Running bent low, rifles blazing, they raced for the shelter of the huge cypresses lining the stream.

Carrying a double-barreled sawed-off shotgun, Bud Sliney dove from a window, rolled to his knees, and took aim at Malinak. Just before Sliney pulled one trigger of the Greener, Jim rose from the creek, thumbed back the hammer of his Peacemaker, and fired. Sliney's aim was ruined, and the load of buckshot peppered the air over Malinak's head when Jim's shot ripped into the gunman's groin. Sliney screamed, throwing aside the shotgun. He grabbed his bullet-torn crotch and went to his knees. Jim dove for the shotgun, grabbed it, and pulled the trigger, sending the second load of buckshot into Sliney's chest. Heart and lungs torn apart by the close-bunched shot, Sliney was slammed to the dirt.

The others had now reached the shelter of the cypresses. They poured a withering fire into the cabin.

Unable to get a good shot at the lawmen, the remaining gunman in the brush emerged from cover for a clear shot at Frank Malinak's back. Malinak grunted and arched backwards from the impact of the bullet striking him low in the back. He toppled against a cypress, slid down its trunk and spun to his belly. McCue spotted the renegade and shot just as he pulled the trigger. The gunman died with Smoky's bullet in his chest.

One more of the outlaws died when he poked his head over a windowsill and Huggins put a bullet into his brain.

"Hold your fire a minute," Jim ordered. He called to the cabin's occupants. "Justin Cox! And whoever's still standin' in there. We've got you surrounded. You've got one chance to give yourselves up. Ten seconds to make up your minds before we blast you to ribbons."

"All right. You win," Cox called back. "There's

three of us in here. We're comin' out. Don't shoot."

"Toss out your guns, then come out with your hands in the air," Jim commanded.

Three men, Cox in the lead, tossed out their guns and emerged from the dogtrot. Still alert, Blawcyzk and McCue started toward them. Suddenly Malinak's Colt roared from where he had fallen, and one last man staggered from behind the cabin, hands clamped to his middle. Malinak pulled himself to his feet, stalked over to the man, and kicked his six-gun out of reach.

"I figured there was one more waitin' to pull a stunt like that," he said.

"Frank! I reckoned you were done for too. I saw that bullet take you in the back," Huggins exclaimed.

"Nah. Just knocked the wind outta me." He twisted his gunbelt around to show where the thick leather had stopped the bullet intended for his spine.

"But what about you, Lieutenant?" he asked Jim. "We thought you were done for when you went down."

"Just an act," Jim answered. "And landin' in that creek made it look even more real. And speakin' of dead, Smoke, I wasn't sure if you'd gotten it just before the shootin' started. Sure sounded like someone did."

"Someone did, but it wasn't me," Smoky

answered. "He's sleepin' real peaceful-like right now. I'll pick him up once these *hombres* are settled."

"Let's tie 'em up," said Jim. "We'll leave 'em until we get the bodies of the rest picked up and loaded on their horses. Then we'll swing by the Circle Bar C, pick up the rest, and head back to Centerville. Cox, this is the end for you. You're facin' a long time in prison, maybe the rest of your life."

"You might think you've won, but you haven't," Cox sneered. "I've got plenty of influence in Austin. I'll make bond within a week. And I won't ever be indicted, let alone tried and convicted."

From behind Jim, Smoky McCue's Colt roared, twice. Cox stood dumbfounded, an expression of complete disbelief on his face. Blood blossomed scarlet on his shirtfront. His mouth opened as if to speak, but he choked on the blood welling from it. He slowly buckled to his knees. A knife slipped from his sleeve, then fell from his hand. Cox's eyes glazed, and he toppled to his face.

"And you said you'd kill me if I shot Cox down, Smoke," Jim said amazed by what had just happened.

Smoky walked over to Cox and picked up the knife.

"And I would've, since that would have been cold-blooded murder. But I reckon he was figurin' on sinking this in your guts, Jim. So I had to shoot him."

"It doesn't matter. Cox was done even if he did get off. His reputation would be ruined no matter what," Huggins said holstering his six-gun. "Saves the state the cost of a trial this way. Now let's finish up here and get back to town. And once we do, you're headed for the doc's, Jim, to get that slug dug outta you. And don't argue with me," he added, before Blawcyzk could object.

"I won't," Jim promised. "Long as I can make one stop first, at the telegraph office. I've got to send wires to headquarters and San Leanna. By now, with the grace of the Good Lord, Julia and Charlie should be home. I need to know that, and to let them know I'm coming home."

"That's a deal," Huggins agreed.

"We'll take care of things here, Jim," Malinak added. "You just take it easy."

"In a minute."

Jim whistled. An answering whinny sounded and a moment later Sizzle, reins trailing, emerged from the brush. He trotted up to Jim, nuzzled his face, then nudged Jim's hip pocket.

"Got one left," Jim said. He dug out a peppermint and slipped it to the horse. Afterwards he went to his saddlebags and dug out a tin of salve and a clean rag.

"I've gotta clean up that bullet wound. You hold still now," he ordered the paint. Sizzle's hide twitched at the sting of the medication, but he stood unmoving while Jim treated the wound. "There. You're all set." Jim patted the gelding's shoulder.

"And you're gonna sit down and rest now or we'll hogtie you, Jim," Smoky threatened.

"All right, I can't fight all of you." Jim conceded. He stretched out against the cabin wall.

The bodies of Justin Cox and his men were loaded onto their horses, tied belly-down over the saddles. Smoky dragged the man he'd knocked unconscious from the brush. Along with the other surviving members of Cox's outfit, once he was mounted his ankles were tied to his stirrups and wrists to the saddle horn.

"We're ready to go, Jim," Smoky said. "It's finally over."

"Not quite. The hardest part's yet to come," Jim answered.

"What do you mean?" Smoky asked, puzzled.

"Facin' Cap'n Trumbull," Jim replied.

Chapter 21

Several days later, Jim reined Sizzle to a momentary stop on the rise overlooking his ranch. Smoke curled lazily from the house's chimney. To his surprise, the pastures were filled with his rustled horses. Even from this height he could make out the buckskin and white markings of Charlie's pet gelding Ted.

"Sure looks peaceful down there, Siz," he said to his horse. "Before we head on in, I just want to say you did a good job, fella. Looks like we'll be ridin' pards for a long time. But now it's time you rest a spell." He patted the big gelding's shoulder. Sizzle nickered a soft response. "Let's get down there. I reckon Julia and Charlie are as anxious to see me as I am them." He lifted the reins and heeled his paint into a jogtrot.

Charlie emerged from the barn carrying a bucket of water just as Jim came through the gate. A collie puppy tagged along at the boy's heels. He spotted the strange rider and commenced a furious barking.

"Dad! Mom! Dad's home!" the boy screamed. He dropped the bucket and ran up to his father. Jim climbed from the saddle. Charlie grabbed him. Jim wrapped his arms around his son in a bear hug while the puppy cavorted around them.

Tears of joy and relief streaked their cheeks.

"Dad, you're home," Charlie repeated. "I sure missed you."

"I missed you too, Charlie. Where's your mom?"

"Inside the house. She's tired and was gonna take a nap. But I'll bet she's wide awake now."

Sam had spotted Jim, and was now pacing frantically in his corral, whinnying insistently to his friend.

"In a few minutes, Sam. I promise," Jim called. "Charlie, how'd our horses get here? And who's your new friend?"

Jim leaned down to scratch the collie pup's ears.

"Joe Walier brought 'em back. He said the circuit judge came into town, started a trial, but the *hombres* who had them confessed before it was over. Our horses weren't needed for evidence, so Joe brought them home. And this is Pal. Mr. Hines brought him over to me after mom and I got back home."

"Okay. Take care of Sizzle for me, will you, Charlie? Rub him down good, then feed and water him."

Jim passed the paint's reins to his son.

"Sure, Dad."

Jim headed for the house, his pace quickening with each step. Just when he reached the stairs the door opened and Julia stepped onto the porch.

He took the steps two at a time, then swept her into his arms. Husband and wife stood for several moments locked in their embrace, swaying gently. Jim finally kissed her, pushed back, and gazed at her face. Only a faint scar under her lip betrayed the ordeal Julia had undergone.

"Julia," he whispered.

"Shh." Julia touched a finger to his lips. "Let me just look at you, Jim. That day everything happened, I believed you were dead. I never thought I would see you again."

"I thought I'd lost you too," Jim answered. "And I was never so scared in my life."

"I want you to hold me, Jim." Julia pleaded. "Please, just hold me."

They took a seat on the porch swing. Jim draped his arm around Julia's shoulder, while she lay her head on his chest. They sat in silence for some minutes, reassured by each other's presence.

Finally, Jim spoke.

"Julia, I want you to know I thought of you every moment I was away from you. I wanted to be here with you so much. But I had to catch the men who hurt you so badly . . . and Charlie. I just couldn't stand being here doing nothing while they were on the loose."

"I know, Jim. And I understand. That isn't to say I wasn't angry at you for leaving me, and hurt. But I also realized you had to do what you did. There's too much Texas Ranger in you. You couldn't have kept from going after those men any more than you could stop breathing. And if you're honest with yourself, you know that while you were thinking of me, you were also being a lawman. But now that you're back home, none of that matters."

"Julia, you're more than I ever deserved," Jim said. "You know me better'n I know myself. No wonder I love you so much." He leaned over and kissed her cheek.

"Is what Tom Justus tells me true? You caught up with those men?" Julia asked. "They won't ever do to another woman what they did to me?"

"I caught them. The man who hurt you worst, Reese Macklin, is in jail over in Cameron, along with two of his men. They'll hang for their crimes. And the man responsible, who paid Macklin to kill me, is dead. So you won't have to worry about them anymore."

Sam was still screaming from his corral. He stood at the gate, pawing the ground.

"Jim, you'd better go see that horse of yours before he tears down the fence," Julia said.

"Are you sure?"

"I'm certain. Just don't take too long."

"I won't," Jim promised. "But I'd better get some peppermints first."

He went into the kitchen to grab some candies, then headed for the corral. Sam shoved his muzzle into Jim's belly, hard, as soon as he entered the

271

enclosure. Jim grunted from the impact. Sam nuzzled Jim's hip pocket for his treat.

"All right, you big beggar, here's your candies." Sam crunched down on the sweets.

"You're lookin' good, fella," Jim told the paint. "Especially considerin' I almost put you down, thinking to end your sufferin'."

As if in answer, Sam galloped around the corral, only a slight limp evident in his stride. He slid to a stop in front of the Ranger, snorting and blowing.

"All right, you're doin' just fine. But I've got to get back to Julia. I'll be back to see you in a bit." He patted Sam's nose and stroked his face.

"You behave," he said, then turned to the gate. Sam clamped his teeth onto Jim's shoulder, pulling him back. "Doggone it horse, let go. We'll have plenty of time later."

Sam released his grip. Jim made two steps toward the gate when Sam grabbed him by the back of his belt, again clamping his teeth down tightly. He pulled hard, dumping Jim on his rear in the dust.

Despite himself, Jim sat there laughing, unable to vent his anger at the gelding. Sam nuzzled the Stetson off Jim's head.

"You're askin' for it, bud," Jim warned. He pushed himself to his feet. Sam clamped his teeth onto Jim's right ear, just enough to hurt.

"Ow! Leggo! That ear's attached, Sam! It don't

come off!" Jim shouted. "You hear me? Let go!"

With a snort, Sam released his grip, then again raced around the corral, bucking and kicking. He ran back up to Jim, reared high and pawed the air, then dropped to all fours.

Jim gazed thoughtfully at his horse. "I think I know what you're tryin' to tell me, ol' pard," he said. "You want to take to the trails again. Well, you sure can't carry me anymore, not with that leg. But if you'll learn to carry a pack saddle, then you'll be able to come along with me and Siz. Seems like you'll be able to keep up. We'll work on that. But for now I've got to return to Julia. I'll come back to say goodnight before we turn in."

Jim returned to where Julia awaited on the porch. He again sat beside her.

"Is Sam settled down?" she asked.

"As much as he'll ever settle down," Jim replied.

"You're two of a kind, you and him. Never content to stay in one place."

"Maybe I finally can."

"You might try and fool yourself, but in a few weeks you'll be itching to go again. And I wouldn't have it any other way. But we're together now. Please hold me like you'll never let go."

Jim and Julia spent the rest of the afternoon in that swing, taking comfort in each other's company. When evening came, they had supper, then again sat on the porch watching the stars come out. At bedtime, Jim stayed with Charlie for quite some time, father and son talking until the boy fell asleep. Except for the bullet scar his chest now bore, Charlie seemed to have recovered completely, both physically and mentally, from his ordeal.

Once he was sure Charlie wouldn't reawaken, Jim headed back to his own bedroom. Julia was already lying there, waiting.

Jim said his prayers, undressed, and slipped into bed alongside his wife. He leaned over to kiss her. When he did, he could feel her cringe, her body tense. She gave a slight shudder.

"Jim, I . . ."

"I know, Julia," Jim whispered. "I know. I'm not trying to rush you into anything. I just want you next to me."

He slid an arm under her shoulders and gently stroked her long, dark hair. Julia snuggled against his side. She looked at the bandage covering the wound along his ribs.

"You got shot again."

"It's nothin'," Jim insisted. "That's why I didn't mention it in my telegram. Didn't want to worry you. You've already been through more'n any woman should have to endure, and I didn't help things by taking after those renegades."

"You're here now and that's all I want," Julia

said. She fingered the bandage, ran her hand over his breast and laid it on his bare chest, content to be at her husband's side once again. Cradled in Jim's arms, she soon was sleeping.

Once Julia fell asleep, Jim lay gazing at the ceiling.

"I know it will be some time before you're ready to make love to me again, Julia," he whispered. "But I can wait. I can wait."

"I can wait the rest of my life if need be," he thought.

Epilogue

After arguing with his two Rangers most of the morning, Captain Hank Trumbull had been glaring over his desk at Jim Blawcyzk and Smoky McCue for a full five minutes. His frosty blue eyes seemed bleak as a snow-swept tundra, his face red with anger. He puffed furiously on his pipe, sending rings of smoke toward the ceiling.

For their parts, Smoky was anxiously puffing on his third cigarette, while Jim returned Trumbull's glare in stony silence. His clear blue eyes were just as icy as the captain's.

Trumbull took one final long pull on his pipe, then spoke again.

"I've read both of your reports. We can argue about this for a month of Sundays and get nowhere. The fact of the matter, Lieutenant Blawcyzk, is that despite my direct orders, you took it upon yourself to track down the men who attacked your ranch. And you wreaked havoc over half of Texas while doin' that. I've got a passel of politicians screamin' at me, breathin' down my neck for the hides of the Rangers who did in Justin Cox. Most of them want my hide too."

"And there's probably just as many who want to shake those Rangers' hands," Smoky muttered.

"I'll have none of your sass, Corporal McCue. You also didn't follow orders. Instead of bringing Jim in you helped him."

"He didn't leave me much choice, Cap'n, unless you'd've preferred I gut-shot him. I figure that would've stopped him, but it seemed a mite drastic at the time."

"Reckon he means you won't be Corporal McCue much longer, Smoke," Jim said. "Probably not even Private McCue."

"Cap'n," he continued, "I can't argue with you. I disobeyed orders, and that's a fact. There's no denyin' it. But what would you have done if you'd been in my boots? Don't bother to answer. I'll answer for you. You'd have done the exact same thing. At least the Hank Trumbull I've always known would have. And don't take it out on Smoky for what I did. He tried to convince me to turn back. I talked him out of it."

"I can just imagine how you 'talked' him out of it," Trumbull snapped. "The fact remains McCue also disobeyed orders. And I've still got to decide what to do about Jim Huggins and Frank Malinak. They didn't make any attempt to stop you either. Instead, they went along with you."

"If they hadn't, Justin Cox would've gotten away with his crimes," Jim said. "They did as they saw fit, Cap'n, just as Rangers in the field are supposed to do. They shouldn't be punished for that."

"Lieutenant, in addition to everything else, there's the matter of your assault on Rangers Timmons and Huggins," Trumbull answered. "I've asked them to be here today to get their statements once again, with you present."

Trumbull stepped to the door.

"Mona, would you send Jeff and Dan in here, please?" he requested.

Moments later, Jeff Timmons and Dan Huggins stepped into the room. Jeff was rolling a quirly, while Dan twisted the Stetson he held.

"Jeff, Dan, take a seat, please," Trumbull invited.

Jeff took a chair in the corner, while Dan settled on the battered couch against the back wall.

"Now, gentlemen, you've already told me what happened at Lieutenant Blawcyzk's ranch on July twenty-ninth," Trumbull said. "But would you mind repeating your stories for his benefit. Jeff, you first please."

Jeff coughed nervously and looked around the room before replying.

"Sure, Cap'n. I was guardin' Jim's place, like you ordered. Dan came by to relieve me, and we decided to practice ropin' and tyin' *hombres*, you know, for when we might take prisoners. Anyway, Dan had tied me up pretty good. Then he left the room for a minute. Next thing I heard was a thud."

"Hold it!" Trumbull exploded. "Now you're

tellin' me it was Dan who hogtied you, not Jim Blawcyzk?"

"Yeah, that's right, Cap'n."

"Seems to me you've changed your story, Timmons. You said before Lieutenant Blawcyzk had pulled a gun on you and tied you up."

"Reckon I was wrong. I was lyin' there tied so long I must've finally passed out from lack of blood circulation. I guess the lack of blood to my brain played tricks with my memory. That must be why I thought the lieutenant had roped me. It was really Dan. When I finally came to he was untyin' me."

"Something's playing tricks with your memory all right," Trumbull protested. "Dan, I suppose now you're gonna tell me you weren't slugged and knocked out by Lieutenant Blawcyzk."

"That's right, Cap'n," Dan answered. "I must've slipped on that Navajo rug Miz' Blawcyzk insists on keepin' in the living room and knocked myself cold, 'cause after I went into that room the next thing I remember is wakin' up with a lump on my head and that rug tangled around my feet. Accordin' to my dad, the lieutenant's always complainin' about that rug bein' dangerous. Seems he's right."

"That's the most ridiculous, unadulterated bunch of bull I've ever heard," Trumbull shouted. "So now you're saying, Ranger Huggins, that Jim Blawcyzk didn't render you unconscious and leave you lyin' at his place while he rode off?"

"That's exactly what I'm saying, Captain."

"I can see what's goin' on here. You're all tryin' to cover up for the lieutenant."

"They'd better not be," Jim interrupted. "Dan, Jeff, I appreciate what you're tryin' to do, but I don't want you lyin' to protect me. Now tell the truth."

"We're not lyin' at all, Jim," Huggins protested. "I slipped and fell on your rug. Then, same as happened to Jeff, that knock on my head must've scrambled my brains for a spell. Things occurred just like we said."

"I won't argue that point about your brains bein' scrambled," Trumbull said frowning.

"Captain, Dan's most likely tellin' the truth about that rug," Smoky interjected. "I've slid on that blasted thing myself. It's a pretty rug but downright hazardous."

"Smoky," Jim growled.

"What?" McCue gave him a withering look.

"Never mind. You *hombres* have your minds made up," Jim shrugged. "But Cap'n, they're lyin' just like that rug. Which no one has ever slipped on, by the way."

"I know that, and it's the first thing I can agree with you on all morning," Trumbull responded. "Look, I've heard enough of this malarkey. I've made my decision. Jim, you know how I feel about you. You've been almost like a son to me. You're also one of the best men ever to ride for the Texas Rangers. Your service to the state has been invaluable. Your sacrifices and those of your family, have been tremendous. But I can't overlook your deliberate disobedience to my orders. Your actions have created many problems for the Rangers that it will take much time and effort to repair. I have to ask for your resignation. I'm sorry."

Jim gasped as if he'd been punched in the gut. He'd expected some repercussions, but to be asked to resign from the Rangers? Stunned, he half-rose from his chair, then fell back, his expression somber. He fingered the badge on his shirt for a moment, slowly unpinned the silver star on silver circle, stared at it, then placed it on Trumbull's desk.

"What about Smoky?" he asked. "He tried to obey your orders, Cap'n, but I wouldn't let him. So he merely did what any good pard would do, went along and helped me best he could. He shouldn't be drummed out for that."

"It don't matter, Jim," Smoky snapped. "If you're not a Ranger, then neither am I." He ripped the badge from his shirt and tossed it alongside Blawcyzk's.

"That goes for me too. I just resigned, Captain," Dan Huggins added.

"Same here," Jeff Timmons put in. "I quit.

Let's head over to the Silver Star and get good and drunk."

"Hold it! There's no need for this," Jim exclaimed. "I appreciate what y'all are tryin' to do, and I'm grateful, but quittin' on my account makes no sense."

"We've made up our minds, Jim," Smoky answered. "You headin' for the Silver Star with us or not?"

"Just wait a minute, all of you," Trumbull ordered. He leaned back in his chair, studying the determined men.

"Perhaps we've all been a bit hasty here," he finally said. "Smoky, Dan, Jeff, your loyalty to Lieutenant Blawcyzk speaks volumes. I'm sure if Jim Huggins and Frank Malinak were here they'd feel the same way."

"I know my dad certainly would," Dan Huggins answered.

"There's something to be said for loyalty and friendship like that. And seeing your affection for Jim, I realize I may have acted too quickly in asking for his resignation. I have to balance everything he's done for the Texas Rangers and the State against this one incident, serious as it might be. I failed to do that."

"You might want to also consider his wife was beaten and raped, his son shot, and Jim himself nearly killed," Smoky added. "That's enough to make any man go a bit loco."

"And don't forget havin' Sam shot and crippled," Jeff added.

"You don't have to stick up for me, Jeff. None of you do," Jim protested.

"We'd better, seein' as you're not doin' a very good job of it yourself," Dan said.

"Just shut up and let the captain speak his piece, Jim, or I'll have to gag you," Smoky ordered.

"All of you just pipe down," Trumbull rumbled. "Jim, obviously your defiance of official orders merits punishment. However, taking into consideration your illustrious service to the State of Texas, I have rethought my decision. I now feel a forced resignation is too harsh a penalty. Instead, would you accept a month's suspension, which I will put in the records as a leave of absence?"

Jim's face broke into a broad grin.

"I sure would, Cap'n. That will give me time with Julia before I have to ride out again. She's still got some tough hurdles ahead. I'd like to be there for her."

"So that's settled," Trumbull said. "I'll have the papers drawn up this morning."

"That's not quite everything," Smoky pointed out. "We all resigned. Are we still Texas Rangers?"

"I don't know," Trumbull grinned. "What do you think, Jim?"

"I think you'd be crazy to let these ornery

cusses join the Texas Rangers, Cap'n," Jim laughed. "But I suppose it's better to have 'em with us than out raisin' Cain on their own."

"Then I don't want to hear any more talk of resignations," Trumbull declared. "Now, let's all head over to the Silver Star. I'll even buy the first round."

"If it's all the same to you, Cap'n, I'd like to get home to Julia and Charlie. They'll be worried," Jim said.

"Of course. But one round of drinks first. And that's an order, Lieutenant."

"Reckon I've got no choice, since it's a direct order." Jim chuckled. "All right, one round. But then I'm headin' home."

"Agreed."

As they headed out the door, Dan questioned Trumbull.

"Hey Cap'n, what about those politicians you said are after yours and the lieutenant's hides? Did you forget about them?"

"Have you ever known me to worry about what some penny-ante politico thinks?" Trumbull thundered.

"Can't say as I have, Cap," Dan responded.

"So you know I can handle them all right. End of discussion."

When they came to where Soot and Sizzle were tied, patiently awaiting their riders, Trumbull stopped in front of Jim's paint. He patted Sizzle's nose. "Sure is a relief bein' able to walk close by your cayuse without havin' to worry about him takin' a chunk out of my hide," he remarked.

Sizzle snorted, dousing Trumbull with spray from his nostrils.

The other Rangers burst into uproarious laughter.

"I never claimed just 'cause Siz doesn't bite it's safe to be around him, Cap'n," Jim said grinning.

"Maybe I'll keep you in the Rangers but not your blamed horse," Trumbull retorted. "C'mon, let's get those drinks."

Jim got out of the Silver Star as quickly as possible. A short time later, he was home. Julia and Charlie were waiting on the porch.

"Well, dad? What happened?" Charlie asked, before Jim could even dismount.

"I'm still a Texas Ranger, Charlie," Jim answered, "But even better, I've got a whole month off to spend with you and your mom."

"Are you sure that's what you want, Jim?" Julia asked. "Staying in one spot for a month will be almost impossible for you?"

Jim swung down off Sizzle's back, climbed the stairs, and enfolded her in his arms.

"I think I can manage," he replied, kissing her full on the lips.

"In fact, I know I can."

About Jim

Jim Griffin became enamored of the Texas Rangers from watching the TV series, "Tales of the Texas Rangers." He grew to be an avid student and collector of Rangers' artifacts, memorabilia and other items. His collection is now housed in the Texas Ranger Hall of Fame and Museum in Waco.

His quest for authenticity in his writing has taken him to the famous Old West towns of Pecos, Deadwood, Cheyenne, Tombstone and numerous others. While Jim's books are fiction, he strives to keep them as accurate as possible within the realm of fiction.

A graduate of Southern Connecticut State University, Jim now divides his time between Branford, Connecticut and Keene, New Hampshire when he isn't travelling around the west.

A devoted and enthusiastic horseman, Jim bought his first horse when he was a junior in college. He has owned several American Paint horses. He is a member of the Connecticut Horse Council Volunteer Horse Patrol, an organization which assists the state park rangers with patrolling parks and forests.

Jim's books are traditional Westerns in the best sense of the term, portraying strong heroes with good character and moral values. Highly reminiscent of the pulp westerns of yesteryear, the heroes and villains are clearly separated.

Jim was initially inspired to write at the urging of friend and author James Reasoner. After the successful publication of his first book, *Trouble Rides the Texas Pacific*, published in 2005, Jim was encouraged to continue his writing. *Ranger's Revenge* is the seventh book in a series of Westerns.

Books are produced in the United States using U.S.-based materials

Books are printed using a revolutionary new process called THINKtech™ that lowers energy usage by 70% and increases overall quality

Books are durable and flexible because of smythe-sewing

Paper is sourced using environmentally responsible foresting methods and the paper is acid-free

Center Point Large Print
600 Brooks Road / PO Box 1
Thorndike, ME 04986-0001 USA

(207) 568-3717

US & Canada:
1 800 929-9108
www.centerpointlargeprint.com